"I want my wife back, the Anna I knew before."

Sebastian's reply came without thought or consideration. Anna suspected it surprised him every bit as much as it did her.

Her hands clenched at her sides. "I don't know who or what Anna is!"

"Don't you?"

So there it was. The first open expression of his disbelief. She'd begun to suspect he doubted her. Here, finally, was the proof. "You don't believe I have amnesia, do you?"

He hesitated. "The possibility that you're faking has crossed my mind."

"Why in the world would I fake something like that? Unless…" She searched his face for a hint to his innermost thoughts. "There's something you haven't told me, isn't there?"

Day Leclaire and her family live in the midst of a maritime forest on a small island off the coast of North Carolina. Despite the yearly storms that batter them, and the frequent power outages, they find the beautiful climate, superb fishing and unbeatable seascape more than adequate compensation. One of the first acquisitions upon moving to Hatteras Island was a cat named Fuzzy. He has recently discovered that laps are wonderful places to curl up and nap—and that Day's son really was kidding when he named the hamster Cat Food.

Books by Day Leclaire

Don't miss any of our special offers. Write to us at the following address for information on our newest releases.

Harlequin Reader Service
U.S.: 3010 Walden Ave., P.O. Box 1325, Buffalo, NY 14269
Canadian: P.O. Box 609, Fort Erie, Ont. L2A 5X3

ONE-NIGHT WIFE
Day Leclaire

Harlequin Books

TORONTO • NEW YORK • LONDON
AMSTERDAM • PARIS • SYDNEY • HAMBURG
STOCKHOLM • ATHENS • TOKYO • MILAN
MADRID • WARSAW • BUDAPEST • AUCKLAND

ISBN 0-373-03376-1

ONE-NIGHT WIFE

First North American Publication 1995.

Copyright © 1995 by Day Totton Smith.

This edition published by arrangement with Harlequin Books S.A.

® and TM are trademarks of the publisher. Trademarks indicated with ® are registered in the United States Patent and Trademark Office, the Canadian Trade Marks Office and in other countries.

Printed in U.S.A.

CHAPTER ONE

"ANNA. Anna, wake up."

"No... Not..." she tried to say, but only a soft moan left her lips.

"Open your eyes, sweetheart. Look at me."

The voice was stark, demanding. Yet she felt a deeper, more powerful emotion underlining the command. Could it be fear? She wanted to resist, to sink back into the welcoming arms of oblivion, but he wouldn't let her.

"Anna!"

She attempted to shake her head. Pain—immediate and acute—stopped her and she held very, very still. "Chris..." She managed to gasp the word, though she didn't quite know why she said it. But just speaking seemed such a triumph, she repeated it. "Chris," she murmured and opened her eyes.

He bent over her, so close he eclipsed all else. She couldn't see him clearly, only a large, blurred outline; her vision refused to focus. "Who's Chris?" he asked sharply.

She couldn't answer... didn't want to answer. The throbbing grew worse, the pain in her head driving out every other thought and consideration and her hand fluttered weakly upward to investigate. But he stopped her, catching her fingers in his and squeezing gently.

"Don't," he warned. "You've injured your head. It's bandaged. But you're all right now. You're safe."

Questions flitted through her mind, slipping in and out of the shadows that fogged her memory, disappearing before she could find the words to express them. Only one remained long enough for her to fix on and she squinted upward, struggling to focus.

"Who are you?" The question exhausted her and her lids drifted closed.

"It's Sebastian." The words were bleak, filled with emotions kept tightly in check. "Your husband."

She fought to gather strength enough to protest, but it was impossible. With a sigh, she gave up the battle, the words dying on her lips...*I don't have a husband*!

The next time she surfaced, she was alone—and without question in a hospital bed. This time no one stopped her when she lifted a hand to her head, investigating the gauze wrapped about her brow. She'd been injured...but *how*? She couldn't remember.

She didn't want to remember.

She lowered her hand, then hesitated, staring at her fingers as a memory stirred. A voice called to her, filled with urgent demand. *Anna!* Then again, the same husky tones, though this time roughened with dark emotion. *It's Sebastian. Your husband.*

She winced. No. That couldn't be right. She wasn't married. No rings decorated her finger, not even a pale mark to suggest she'd ever worn a wedding band. Or had she?

For just a moment, an image burst to life. She remembered hearing a tremendous crack of thunder and then a blinding flash of lightning caught on a pair of rings. They arched through midair, blazing with blue fire—diamonds in a platinum setting—captured for a split second by the harsh white light as they tumbled over and over.

She stirred restlessly. She had to leave. The realization came to her, absolute and unquestionable. She had to go now before . . . before . . . Before what? The memory flitted just out of reach, tantalizing, drifting ever closer. And she knew without any doubt that should she remember, it would put into motion a chain of events she'd be helpless to avert. And she didn't want that to happen.

There was only one option available. She'd bury the memories. Bury them so they'd never hurt her again.

This time when she regained consciousness, the pain had subsided and she felt much stronger. She looked around carefully, examining her surroundings. Blinds covered the windows beside the bed, the slats adjusted to allow only a tempered amount of the bright sunshine to filter into the room, giving everything a shadow-washed appearance. A huge basket of flowers overflowed the top of a nearby dresser and a gauzy white curtain surrounded much of the bed, billowing lazily in the soft, warm breeze that slipped in from the window. A paper rustled, catching her attention, and she turned her head toward the sound.

And that's when she saw him.

He sat in a chair at her side, engrossed in a copy of *The Wall Street Journal.* He'd been with her when she'd first been admitted to the hospital, she vaguely recalled. He'd spoken to her, told her his name. She bit down on her lip, struggling to remember. But the name eluded her.

She studied him curiously. Thick black hair curled with stubborn abandon about a toughly hewn face—a face well accustomed to the sun and salt air. A nearly invisible scar slashed a silvery path from the corner of his right eye to the top of his lip, giving his mouth a tilted, half-laughing, half-taunting expression and marring otherwise perfect features.

She frowned. No. Not marring. The paper-thin scar lent character, offered enticing fantasies of pirates and buccaneers and danger. How had he received the injury? she couldn't help but wonder. An accident? A fight? A jealous lover?

One thing she knew for certain. She'd never seen this man before in her life. His wasn't a face easily forgotten. If she'd ever met him, she'd remember. The newspaper rustled again as he turned the page, and she realized that as curious as she was about the man, she couldn't just lay here and stare at him. She had questions that demanded answers.

"Excuse me," she interrupted quietly. Her voice sounded odd, husky and unfamiliar, as though she hadn't used it for a long time. "I wonder if you could help me."

He froze, then slowly lowered the paper, and she found herself gazing into eyes the precise color of a stormy winter sky. He studied her with a compelling intensity she couldn't mistake, turbulent emotions reflected in his searching scrutiny. For one tense moment, nothing stirred, as though time itself held its breath. Then a deliberate calm settled across his tautly carved features, wiping away all expression.

"Anna," he said in a deep, cool voice. "It's good to see you awake. How do you feel?"

Her brow crinkled. He'd called her Anna. Which meant even if she didn't know *him*, he knew *her*. But, Anna? The name felt as alien to her as he did. Could he have confused her with someone else? A hint of unease stirred. If that were true... If Anna wasn't her name... then what was? Her breathing grew shallow and rapid as she searched frantically for an answer.

"Anna?" He spoke sharply, dragging her attention from her scattered thoughts. "Are you all right?"

"No. No, I'm not all right." A torrent of questions pressed for release. Who are you? How do you know me? Why don't I know anything, remember anything? *Who am I?*

He crushed the newspaper in his fist. "What's wrong? Are you in pain?"

"Where am I?" she questioned tautly.

"In a hospital in south Florida."

"What happened to me?"

A frown pulled his thick, winged brows together. "You were injured in a car accident."

"When?"

"Two days ago."

"How badly?"

"Not bad, all things considered. Concussion." He gestured toward her head. "You've a stitch or two under that bandage. Bruises, scrapes." A muscle jerked in his jaw. "It's a miracle you weren't killed."

He waited, as though expecting her to offer an explanation—and she knew she couldn't delay the inevitable any longer. She took a deep breath. "I should know you, shouldn't I?" she said.

He stilled, his gaze piercing, the gray darkening to a deep pewter. He didn't say anything for several impossibly long minutes. "Are you saying you don't?" he questioned at last.

Reluctantly, she shook her head. "I'm afraid not."

He tossed the crushed newspaper aside in an abrupt, sweeping motion. "Is this your idea of a joke?"

Her grip tightened on the bedsheet. "It's not a joke."

"You're saying you don't know me?"

"No, I don't." She gathered every ounce of fortitude she possessed, and admitted, "I...I don't even know who I am."

He thrust back his chair and stood. Crossing to the window, he stared out for an endless moment before glancing over his shoulder. The sun streaked across his face, emphasizing the lines of fatigue that marked his brow and the sides of his mouth. But it was his eyes that held her attention. Caught by the bright sunshine they glittered a pale silvery-gray, blazing with anger and suspicion. He turned to confront her, putting the sun at his back so that his face fell into shadow.

"I'm your husband. Sebastian," he informed her, folding his arms across his chest. "And you're Anna Kane...my wife."

His reply struck a cord. In the far recesses of her mind, his voice drifted to her. "*It's Sebastian. Your husband*."

"No! No, that's not possible. I'm not married." She loosened her hold on the sheet and held out her left hand. "See? No rings. Not even a mark."

He made a small sound of annoyance. "It won't work, Anna," he bit out. "I don't know what game you're playing, but you're deluding yourself if you think I'll play along."

"It's not a game," she protested.

"Isn't it?"

"No!"

"You can't escape the repercussions with this little act." He ran a hand through his hair, irritation edging his words. "Damn it, Anna. What were you thinking? Why did you leave like that? And who the *hell* is Chris?"

She winced at the sudden, stabbing pain in her head. "I don't know any Chris."

"You spoke his name," he argued, his skepticism unmistakable. "When they first brought you here, you called to him. You must know who he is."

"Well, I don't," she repeated.

She could feel him weighing her response, watching her with nerve-racking intensity. "I would have bet my life you'd never resort to deception," he murmured. "But then ... the past two days have taught me a lot."

"Please," she said, raising a hand to her brow. The pressure built, her headache returning with a vengeance. "I can't answer your questions. I don't *know* the answers."

She could feel his impatience. He approached the bed, his shoulders impossibly wide beneath the thin cotton of his shirt. She gazed at him in alarm, not quite certain what he intended. To her consternation, he sat on the edge of the mattress as though it were his right and gathered her hands in his. They were long-fingered and capable. Strong hands, calloused hands.

"Anna, look at me," he ordered softly. "We can work this out. Just tell me what the problem is."

She stared at him in confusion, struggling to make sense of a senseless situation. "I'm telling you the truth. I don't know you. Why don't you believe me?" The throbbing intensified and she closed her eyes, too exhausted to argue further.

"You're in pain again," he said with swift awareness. "I'll get the doctor."

He released her hands and stood, his footsteps fading in the distance. But the blessed solitude lasted only a fleeting moment. Almost immediately he returned with the nurse and a short, balding man she assumed must be her doctor.

He didn't waste any time confirming her guess. "I'm Dr. Tellbeck, Mrs. Kane," he began in soothing tones. "Your husband mentioned you're having a small memory lapse."

She glanced at Sebastian. *Her husband*. The term seemed so strange, so foreign. Was it possible? Could he really be her husband? It seemed inconceivable she'd forget something so significant. She searched his face, praying she'd sense even a vague familiarity. But there was nothing. Nothing but an instinctive knowledge that something about this whole situation was very, very wrong.

"I don't remember anything," she said, her eyes drooping.

"Are you in pain?" the doctor probed gently.

She started to nod, then winced. He turned and murmured something to the nurse, who promptly disappeared from the room. A moment later she returned with a small tray. "This will help you sleep, Mrs. Kane," Dr. Tellbeck informed her, removing a syringe from the tray. "With a few days' rest, I suspect your memory will return. In the meantime, we'll run

a few tests, just to be positive nothing's been overlooked." A needle pricked her arm. Instantly she felt
an odd floating sensation and her mind began to drift.

"Bring in a specialist," she heard Sebastian order,
his voice muffled, as though coming from a long distance. "A neurologist. Money's no object. I want the
best."

"Of course, Mr. Kane."

"What about visitors?" the nurse questioned.
"There's a gentleman who's been asking to see her."

"Who?" Sebastian demanded. "What's his
name?"

"Why... he didn't say."

"No one is permitted in this room without my express authorization," Sebastian stated implacably. "In
the morning I'll make arrangements to move my wife
to a private clinic."

The room began to roll like the deck of a ship on
a stormy sea and Anna's gaze clung to the only stable
object—Sebastian. She could feel his concern, fierce
and primitive and elemental, and she didn't dare look
away. If she did, she knew without a doubt she'd be
lost to the darkness creeping ever closer.

In that instant everything changed. It was as though
time spun in a crazy kaleidoscope. She could still see
Sebastian, but he'd changed. His hair brushed his
shoulders in thick, tight curls, a red scarf banding his
forehead. A thin, linen shirt fell open to his waist,
revealing a broad, muscular chest furred with crisp,
dark hair. And his eyes... His eyes were no longer
gray, but as black as a night sky.

And in his hand he held a pirate's cutlass.

"No," she whispered. "It's not possible."

In response, Sebastian took a step toward her, his expression full of determination. With a moan, she closed her eyes, allowing the darkness to consume her.

The next three days passed in quick succession, and though she improved physically, her memory didn't return. Sebastian installed her in a small, private clinic, claiming it would enable her to receive the best possible medical care, but she couldn't help wondering if there weren't another reason for the move—like the stranger who had attempted to visit her in the hospital.

It was a disturbing notion.

What little she managed to see of this new facility astonished her with its sheer opulence. Fabric wallpaper in a dusky rose wash covered the walls of her room, a private suite that contained all the modern conveniences—TV, VCR, stereo and CD player. The room was large and airy, with a sitting area and dining facilities situated at one end. Even the bathroom was state-of-the-art, furnished with perfumed soaps, a hair-dryer, curling iron and thick, fluffy towels and robes. She might have been in the most exclusive of hotels instead of a medical facility.

Her days consisted of tests and more tests, her nights filled with boredom. On her fourth day at the clinic they permitted her to shower without assistance and she found it pure bliss. Afterward, she slipped on yet another fresh nightgown—this one in a cheerful lemon-yellow with a matching robe. It would seem she had an endless supply of these modest, ankle-length cotton gowns and robes, though they looked and felt as foreign to her as everything else.

A brief rap sounded on the bathroom door and she opened it to discover Sebastian standing there. "More tests?" she guessed with an unhappy sigh. "Give me a minute. I'd like to finish drying my hair."

He braced his shoulder against the jamb, filling the doorway, gentle wisps of steam swirling past him. "No hurry. And no more tests. You're done with them as far as I'm concerned."

"Thank goodness for that." She swiped at the smoked mirror with a hand towel and peeked at her image with notable reluctance.

He tilted his head to one side. "What's wrong?"

A rueful smile tilted her mouth. "It's disconcerting," she admitted with a shrug. "It's like looking at a stranger."

He lifted an eyebrow in disbelief, moving to stand directly behind her. The spacious bathroom seemed to shrink, but there was nowhere to retreat—assuming she cared to retreat.

"You don't even recognize your own appearance?" he asked.

She fixed her attention on her reflection. Large, golden-brown eyes with ridiculously long dark lashes dominated a heart-shaped face. Her glance shifted to lock with his. "Not at all," she told him with a false calm, her gaze unflinchingly direct. "I don't even remember how I wore my hair."

A small frown creased his brow and then his hands closed on her shoulders, squeezing reassuringly. "Well, I remember," he stated quietly, and picked up her brush.

He applied himself to the task with a practiced familiarity that amazed her. Her hair, straight and slightly longer than shoulder-length, slipped through his fingers like silk, the wispy bangs helping to hide the tiny row of bandaged stitches at her temple. An interesting shade between blond and brown, the strands were highlighted with streaks of bright gold.

She stared as he worked the brush through her hair, mesmerized. It never ceased to amaze her that this man was her husband. On one hand, she was desperate to cling to the connection, to have someone to whom she belonged. But on the other hand, an odd wariness urged that she maintain a certain distance, an unanswerable question overriding every other consideration...

How could she possibly be married to the man and have no memory of their time together, no memory of having loved him, having been held in his arms and kissed by him, having shared the deepest, most passionate of intimacies? She couldn't believe she'd forget such a vital piece of her life.

"You've done this before," she commented in a low voice, shaken by the level of intimacy it suggested.

He returned the brush to the counter. "Once or twice," he confirmed, his hands settling on her shoulders. "Now what do you see?"

She glanced in the mirror again, pleased with the casual style. It framed her face, making the most of her bone structure. "I see a woman of about twenty-two with well-brushed hair."

His husky laugh stirred the air. "You see a woman of twenty-four with well-brushed hair."

She wrinkled her nose. "Oh, dear. That old?"

"Robbing the cradle has never appealed to me. I prefer women with some depth and experience." His hands tightened. "Go on. What else do you see?"

She considered. "The features aren't bad," she decided after a moment's thought. "If you don't mind the mole."

He slid his hand beneath her chin, his thumb brushing across the small dark mole that rode high on her left cheekbone. "It's a very kissable feature," he assured her.

A flush swept across her face, his comment catching her by surprise. "I'll take your word for it. But..."

"But what?"

She tilted her head to one side. "But I'm not quite the type of woman one would expect to find married to a man like you."

"No?" His eyes narrowed. "And what type of woman would that be?"

"Glamorous. Sophisticated." She shrugged. "I can hardly claim those particular traits."

"Perhaps there were other traits I considered more important."

"Such as?"

"Look in the mirror. It's all there."

She took a deep breath and followed his instruction, struggling to see beneath the surface. It wasn't easy. "What should I be looking for?" she asked.

"A proud, stubborn chin. A painful directness lurking about the eyes. An easy smile that suggests a good sense of humor."

"You see all that?" she demanded, taken aback.

"I used to."

She stiffened. "But you don't anymore?"

He didn't answer, his silence a far more speaking response. "It's time we had a talk."

His announcement didn't surprise her. She'd anticipated the need for this conversation for days now. Sebastian had remained amazingly quiet since her accident, limiting their discussions to the mundane. Waiting, it seemed... Always waiting. For her memory to return? she couldn't help but wonder. For the doctor to find a physical cause for her amnesia? Or had he deliberately chosen to avoid the subject of their past—and their future—for reasons of his own? It would seem that the time had come for answers to those questions.

"We could go into the sitting area," she suggested.

"I didn't plan on having our discussion in the bathroom," he assured dryly. "There's a central courtyard that offers more privacy. We'll go there. But first I'll need to get a wheelchair for you."

She turned to face him. "A wheelchair?" she protested. "Is that really necessary? I feel fine."

"The administration insists on it for safety reasons. Finish up in here and I'll be back in a few minutes."

He left her then and she picked up the hairbrush, staring at it blindly. Now that the moment had come, she wasn't certain she wanted to hear what he had to say. She couldn't escape the instinctive sense that something was out of kilter. That feeling of "wrongness" had returned full force.

She heard movement in the bedroom, and assuming Sebastian had returned, started to open the door. Two staff workers were busy making her bed, talking quietly. Anna froze as she realized just what they were discussing.

"Are you sure? He hired a private investigator?" one questioned skeptically. "Why would he do that?"

"Probably because he doesn't believe she has amnesia any more than the doctors do. I'll bet he wants the detective to check out her story. And I get the feeling there was something very odd about that accident of hers."

Anna drew back, her heart pounding. Dear heavens, was it true? Had Sebastian hired a private investigator to look into the crash...to investigate her? *Why*?

They finished the bed and moved to straighten the sitting area, their remarks reaching her with stunning clarity. "Well, he obviously doesn't trust her. Why else would he have standing orders that she isn't to leave the room unattended? I think it's to make sure she doesn't run off."

"Really? Could be. That would explain why she isn't allowed any visitors. Maybe she has a secret lover he's trying to keep her from."

The other laughed, moving toward the door. "Or maybe she has a not-so-secret lover he's trying to keep her from!"

And with that, they were gone.

Dear Lord, what was going on? Anna covered her mouth with her hand, all her earlier doubts returning with a vengeance. Her instincts hadn't misled her. Something was seriously wrong. Her first impulse was to rush out into the hallway, track Sebastian down and demand answers. But the urge swiftly passed. She needed to think. To consider her options.

Opening the bathroom door, she crossed to the small kitchenette and poured herself a glass of orange juice. Her fingers trembled, juice splashing onto the spotless counter. She set the carton down and closed her eyes, fighting for control. *Calm down*! she ordered sternly. There was some mystery surrounding her accident, that much was clear, as well as concern about the stranger who'd attempted to contact her in the hospital. All she had to do was ask Sebastian. Ask him flat out about their past... about the accident.

She opened her eyes. *About their marriage*.

The orange juice helped relax her. But it took all her focus and concentration to steel herself for the coming discussion. Considering the nervous flutter in her stomach, she suspected she didn't care much for confrontations. Nor had Sebastian mentioned anything about her being courageous when he'd listed her various personality traits. She frowned as she rinsed her glass. Well... since she didn't know whether or not she possessed that particular characteristic, she'd simply have to proceed as though she did. Proud, stubborn and foolishly courageous. Accurate or not, it was a start.

"Anna?" Sebastian called, pushing a wheelchair into the room. "Are you ready?"

She turned to face him, taking a deep breath. "Yes, I'm ready."

He approached, his gray eyes cool and watchful. "Good. Then let's go."

Before she realized what he intended, he scooped her up, deposited her in the wheelchair, and without another word, pushed her into the marble-floored hallway. The clinic was lovely, potted plants clustered in each corner, skylights flooding the hallway with brilliant sunshine. Still, Anna disliked it on sight. Nothing could hide the fact that it was a medical retreat for the very wealthy, designed to pamper the most exacting of tastes and the most exotic ailments—regardless of whether those ailments were real, imaginary or brought about by an indulgence in a too fast, self-destructive life-style.

Eventually they wound their way toward the center of the clinic, which had been built around an impressively large arboretum. They entered the courtyard through automatic doors, leaving behind the sterile, air-conditioned coolness for the contrasting warmth and humidity of the outdoors. Anna closed her eyes and lifted her face to the warm rays of the sun. For the first time in days, she filled her lungs with fresh air. It was such a simple thing, and yet it was a delight that threatened to bring tears to her eyes.

Sebastian parked the chair by the entrance and set the brake. "I think it's safe to ditch this thing," he said, offering her his hand. "Let's walk."

After a brief hesitation, she slipped her fingers in his, too happy to escape the chair to reject his help. To her relief, he seemed in no hurry. They wandered down various slate-lined pathways where little nooks with benches and wrought-iron tables and chairs were set among the brilliant flowering plants and bushes. Though currently deserted, Anna guessed their colorful arrangement had been designed to please while at the same time screening for privacy.

"Your mood's changed," he commented, breaking the silence between them. "What's wrong?"

She didn't look at him, keeping her gaze trained on the circuitous path ahead. "You mean . . . aside from the fact that I have amnesia and the man who claims to be my husband is a complete stranger to me?"

Her phrasing didn't escape his notice. "Claims to be?" he repeated softly.

Did he sense her growing tension? she wondered. Probably. "If you hadn't told me, I wouldn't know my own name." She shot him a quick look and added, "If you hadn't told me, I wouldn't even know I had a husband."

"Then it's fortunate I'm here to remind you."

He stopped to pluck a brilliant red hibiscus blossom from a heavily laden bush. Drawing her close, he slid it behind her left ear, his thumb caressing the small mole on her cheekbone. The gentle touch came naturally, spontaneously, as though he'd done it a hundred times before.

"Perhaps we could find some way to refresh your memory," he murmured. "Something the doctors might not have considered."

She pulled back, suspecting she knew what he had in mind. "I don't think so," she said, rejecting the idea without bothering to hear what it might be. "We're here to talk, remember?"

"And we will." His grip tightened and he eased her back into his arms, slipping her into the cradle of his hips. "But first things first."

Without giving her time to draw breath, let alone argue, he lowered his head and brushed her mouth with his. It was a fleeting caress, nothing that should have stirred the fierce, primitive reaction that swept through her.

But it did.

She broke free of his hold and turned away, her robe flaring out around her and catching in the thorns of a rosebush. Without a word, he reached down and released her. She didn't hesitate, but continued down the path, deeper into the maze of shrubbery, not bothering to wait and see if he followed. She needed time to recover her equilibrium. She especially needed time to gather whatever courage she might possess and ask the question uppermost on her mind.

Inevitably, she reached a dead end, a sun-dappled bench blocking the path. Gathering the voluminous skirt of her nightgown and robe in one hand, she settled onto the padded bench and drew a deep breath. The hibiscus blossom tumbled free of her hair and landed on the slate walkway at her feet.

Sebastian approached, his footsteps measured and deliberate. Stopping in front of her, he bent and scooped up the bruised flower, staring down at it for a long, endless minute. Then he lifted his gaze to hers. "What is it, Anna?" he asked quietly. "What's wrong?"

The time for truth had come. It was time for some answers. Answers only he could provide. "Tell me, Sebastian. Tell me honestly," she said. "Are you really my husband?"

CHAPTER TWO

SEBASTIAN'S hand closed around the hibiscus blossom. "You don't believe I'm your husband?" he demanded, tossing the flower aside. "Why the sudden doubts? What the hell is going on, Anna?"

"Anyone in my predicament would have the same doubts," she retorted. "It's perfectly understandable. I don't remember you. I don't remember our marriage." She gestured to indicate her nightgown. "I don't even remember the clothes I'm wearing."

His mouth curved with wry amusement and he settled on the bench next to her. "You don't remember your clothes, my love," he informed her with a gently mocking expression, "because the nightgowns are new."

"Then where are *my* things?" she wanted to know. "Why haven't you brought them? Maybe they would help me remember, spark a memory or something."

He slipped a hand along her jaw and beneath the silken sweep of her hair. "I didn't bring any nightwear because you don't wear any."

She inhaled sharply, her eyes wide and shocked. "I don't believe you. You're making that up."

"It's the truth." His voice was dark and husky and laced with an intimacy she longed to challenge. And yet...and yet he spoke with such conviction, with such undeniable certainty. "We slept in each other's

24

arms as nature intended—with nothing to separate us.''

She shook her head. "No. You're lying."

"Am I? Then hear more of my lies. Listen while I tell you how it was between us." His thumb followed the curve of her jaw, inflaming the nerve-endings with each teasing caress. "Shall I begin with the long days of passion we shared? They were days of rapture and discovery that slipped past in the mere flicker of an eyelash. Entire days when we discarded our clothing and our inhibitions and came together with all the blaze and fury of a summer storm."

"Stop it," she ordered, attempting to pull away. "I don't want to hear this."

He refused to release her. "You will hear. You'll hear about the sweet nights when exhaustion claimed us. When you lay in my bed with your head on my shoulder and your mouth pressed to my chest."

"This isn't what I wanted to discuss with you," she protested.

"No?" He held her so close she could feel the heat of his body through the thin cotton of her nightgown and robe. So close she could see the turbulent play of emotions that darkened his eyes to pewter. "You're the one with doubts. I'm just trying to settle them for you."

"By seducing me?" She shook her head. "You aren't going to resolve my doubts that way. Can't you understand? I have no way of knowing whether or not we're really married."

He stilled. "You have my word."

"Perhaps that's not enough," she said quietly, the conversation she'd overheard underscoring her reservations.

"No?" His fingers brushed her lips before tracing the long, graceful curve of her neck. "If it's all a fabrication, then why does your body react to mine with such heat? I can feel your pulse pounding beneath my hand. And when you look at me, your eyes are soft and dark with need, your skin flushed with desire. Did you think I wouldn't notice? Your body remembers me, even if you don't."

"That isn't desire," she claimed, struggling to rationalize her response. "I'm angry, not excited."

A faint laugh escaped him. "You're fooling yourself, if that's what you believe."

She drew back and to her relief, his hands fell away. She couldn't think straight when he touched her. And she needed to think, to gather her defenses and apply logic instead of emotion to this impossible situation. "I'm not certain what the truth is," she began. "But I know there's more to this than meets the eye."

The abrupt change in his expression totally unnerved her. His face hardened, the passion that had marked his angled features only moments before draining away. "You *know*?" he repeated softly. "If you have amnesia, how is it possible to be so sure?"

His comment caught her by surprise. All this time, she'd been the one questioning everything, demanding proof that he was who he'd claimed, that they were married. Now he'd turned the tables on her with a vengeance. For the first time she realized she wasn't the only one with doubts. *He didn't believe she'd lost her memory*! She could read the suspicion in his eyes, hear it in his voice. But...why in the world would he think such a thing?

She looked at him, undaunted. "What are you suggesting, Sebastian?"

"You claim to know there's more going on than meets the eye. Why?" He leaned forward. "Has your mind cleared? Have you made a sudden, miraculous recovery?"

She didn't dare lie, his reaction forcing her to be honest. "No," she admitted. "I haven't remembered anything."

"Then why do you question what I tell you? Why do you suspect we're not married?"

A telltale warmth heated her cheeks. "Because I can't believe I'd forget something so important. Wouldn't I sense it, if we'd been . . . been . . ."

"Lovers?"

Her gaze flashed to his. "Intimate! And we haven't been."

"You're so certain?"

She stared over his shoulder at the pale pink oleander towering behind him. Was she certain? Without a memory or a past, all she had to rely on were her instincts—instincts which had warned from the beginning that something about their relationship was off balance. When she'd first awakened she'd been so certain she wasn't married. And then there was that horrible conversation she'd overheard . . .

She took a deep breath. "You say we're married, but for some reason it feels . . . wrong," she stated without equivocation. "I don't remember you, or our marriage, not even my own name. You don't have a clue how frightening it is to wake up and have your mind empty, every last memory wiped clean as though it had never been. Is it any wonder that I question everything—including our relationship?"

A muscle jerked in his cheek. "You are my wife, and by heaven, it's time you remembered that much, at least." He slid his hands down her spine and brought her close. "Every time I've touched you, you've reacted. So perhaps this will help recover your memory."

She knew what he intended, could read it in the resolute lines marking his expression. "Sebastian, please! This isn't necessary."

His mouth firmed. "I think it's very necessary."

He cupped her face between his hands and gazed down at her. Slowly she relaxed, mutely bending to his will. Perhaps he was right. Perhaps allowing the embrace would help prove...or disprove...his claims. Perhaps another simple kiss would give her the answers she so desperately sought.

Unfortunately, this kiss was far from simple.

His lips stole over hers with a sensuality that caught her completely off guard, lingering, teasing...and decimated any hint of resistance. She allowed the kiss, curious to gauge the effect. What she hadn't anticipated was the strength of her reaction, a helpless, urgent, thundering response that didn't allow for caution or hesitation.

Every thought splintered, opposition replaced by a strange yearning to explore all he had to offer. With a soft moan of surrender, her head fell back and her lips parted beneath the persuasive pressure of his. He took instant advantage, kissing her with a depth and passion that stripped her of all defenses. It was as though he intended to stamp her with his possession so thoroughly, she'd never again forget she'd known his embrace.

"Do you still have doubts about who I am?" he muttered against her mouth. "Does your response tell you nothing?"

"It tells me you're experienced." She drew in a ragged breath. "Very experienced."

"If that's all you can say, then I haven't accomplished my goal."

Again he took her mouth, the quality of the kiss changing, becoming more urgent, more demanding. It was as though his touch tapped into some secret part of her soul, fed a need she hadn't even realized existed. She submitted without hesitation, unable—or willing—to give proper consideration to the consequences. She only knew that to push him away would be more painful than to yield.

Yield? She groaned quietly. She'd done far more than merely yield to his embrace. Her wholesale capitulation had been as spontaneous as it was fervent. "Sebastian . . . Please, don't do this to me. Not now. Not like this. Not when I'm so confused."

"You will remember me, Anna," he told her with unmistakable tenderness. "And it will be here and now. I swear by all I hold dear, I'll find a way to get through to you."

Before she could regain her sanity sufficiently to pull away, he released the buttons of her robe, easing his hands beneath and slipping the covering down her shoulders to expose the thin cotton nightgown. She couldn't think, couldn't draw strength enough to protest.

He pulled back slightly, staring down at her, and she knew she should stop him, that she should end this now. Because she was totally unprepared to deal with the aftermath should she allow him to go any further—should she allow him to strip away any more of her defenses? She grasped his wrists, discovering that they were as solid and inflexible as tree trunks.

"Sebastian, please," she whispered.

"Don't fight me, Anna," he urged. "Not now. Not when you want it as much as I do."

She gave way beneath his insistence. With a gentle hand he explored the soft curves he'd uncovered, his touch as light as a feather, his bronzed skin a stark contrast to the pale butter-yellow of her gown.

She shivered, gazing at him through half-closed eyes. His face was marked with sharp hunger, the skin pulled taut across the chiseled planes of his cheekbones. The color of his eyes had deepened to a shade of gray so dark they were almost black. She slid her hands up his arms, the tense muscles beneath her palms like braided cords of iron rather than mere flesh and bone and sinew. She couldn't hide the desire that inflamed her. Nor could she give in to it.

Just as she thought her control would snap, he released her, sinking his hands deep into her hair and feathering her tender mouth with a final, gentle salute. And of all that had gone before, that one brief caress proved to be the most shattering.

"Bastian," she whispered against his mouth, aching for a possession she knew could never be...should never be.

He gripped her upper arms and thrust her away. "You *do* know me. Don't lie! Admit the truth."

"I—I don't understand," she protested, shocked by his reaction. "I've already told you the truth. As far as I'm aware, I don't know you."

Suspicion glittered in his eyes and she wondered what she'd done to warrant such a violent reaction. Had she been too responsive? As much as she hated to admit it, she couldn't have prevented her surrender to him any more than she could have kept the sun from rising in the sky.

His mouth compressed and his grip eased. "Well, you may not know me, but your body sure as hell does."

Her eyes dropped before his probing gaze. "We're not strangers," she conceded at last.

"Not strangers?" He lifted an eyebrow, dry amusement lacing his words. "Admit it, Anna. Admit that at the very least, we've been lovers."

"Why are you pushing this?" His expression closed over with a speed that took her by surprise, and she drew back. There was something else going on here. Something she'd missed. Something besides an uncomplicated, husbandly embrace. Her brows drew together in bewilderment. If only she could figure out what it might be. "I don't understand what game you're playing, but I will. You can count on it," she informed him.

"You're the one playing games," came his instant reply. "I felt the effect I had when I held you...kissed you. You can protest all you want, but it was there, nonetheless."

"And I haven't denied it," she retorted with as much dignity as she could muster. "But that doesn't mean you're my husband."

"No? Then what does it mean?"

She'd rather not think about that. The possibilities made her far too uncomfortable. In one fluid movement, she stood and drew her robe up her arms. She fastened the small pearl buttons at her throat as though the act alone could negate the tumultuous moments she'd spent in his arms. If nothing else, it helped her face him with a shred of composure.

"I suppose it means that you're good at seducing women," she said.

He lifted an eyebrow. "You've changed since the accident," he commented. "I don't care for it."

"Considering I have no idea how I was before, there's not much I can do about that." She made a sweeping gesture. "I am what I am. What more do you want from me?"

"I want my wife back, the Anna I knew before." The reply came without thought or consideration. And she suspected it surprised him every bit as much as it did her.

Her hands clenched at her sides. "I don't know who or what that Anna is!"

"Don't you?"

So there it was. The first open expression of his disbelief. She'd begun to suspect he doubted her. Here, finally, was the proof. "You want me to be frank?" she questioned tightly. "Very well, I will be. You don't believe I have amnesia, do you?"

He hesitated. "The possibility that you're faking has crossed my mind."

"Why in the world would I fake something like that? It's ridiculous. Unless…" She searched his face for a hint to his innermost thoughts, but she might as well have tried to summon a reaction from the craggy surface of a stone. "There's something you haven't told me, isn't there?"

He leaned back against the bench, watching her closely. "Is there?"

She caught her bottom lip between her teeth. "What is it? Was our marriage unhappy?"

He shook his head. "I told you how it was between us, though it pleases me to hear you concede there was a marriage. Or is your loss of memory a pretense after all? A small slip, Anna?''

"I'm not conceding anything,'' she retorted, stung. "Nor is my amnesia a pretense. How could you even think such a thing? Since you refuse to fill in the details, I'm merely exploring the various possibilities.''

"And one of those possibilities is that we were unhappy? Interesting that you'd leap to that particular conclusion. Why is that, I wonder?''

She clasped her hands together, almost pleading with him. "If you believe I'm faking, there has to be a reason. So, tell me. Was I? Was I unhappy with you?''

But he wouldn't relent. "No, Anna. I won't let you reduce it to such simplistic terms.''

She gazed at him in concern. What secrets were masked by those odd, silvery-gray eyes? she couldn't help but wonder. Whatever they were, he kept them well-hidden. "It's precisely that simple. Either our life together—the life you claim we had—was a delight or a disaster. All I'm asking is which it was.''

He came off the bench in one lithe move, his hands closing about her upper arms and drawing her close. "Judge for yourself. You know how it felt to be in my arms. You trembled when I kissed you, came alive beneath my hands. Did it feel like a disaster to you?''

"Earthquakes are disasters, aren't they?'' she muttered. For the earth had surely rocked beneath her feet when he'd held her, when he'd kissed her. Her comment amused him, she could tell. A broad smile creased his mouth, the sheer beauty of it stealing the breath from her lungs.

"Is that how it felt? Like an earthquake had rumbled underfoot, ripping your life apart?''

"Is that how it was for you?" she countered.

His smile faded and she suspected he had indeed experienced a jolt or two. Did he resent the sensations she'd unwittingly aroused? Would he have preferred to remain immune to them? It wouldn't surprise her. He struck her as the type who needed to remain in total control. And what they'd experienced hadn't left much room for control.

"You're a beautiful woman, Anna. A passionate woman. There'd be something seriously wrong with any man who didn't lose his head a little when he made love to you. And for your information..." He caught her chin with his index finger, tilting her head so the sunlight spilled across her face like liquid gold. "If we'd been anywhere else but here, you'd have known my possession."

"No!"

"No?" He laughed, a soft, husky sound that stirred the air between them with stormy turbulence. "Who's kidding who? You can't even meet my eyes when you lie, can you?"

Her gaze flew to his, faltering beneath the blatant heat she read there. "You haven't answered my question," she managed to say. "Was our marriage a disaster?"

His hands shifted, settling distressingly close to her breasts. "After what you experienced today, can you honestly suspect you were dissatisfied as my wife?"

"I don't know." His hands tightened, warning that he wouldn't let her get away with such a vague response. She sighed. "All right, no. I probably wasn't dissatisfied. At least not that way. But—"

"Stop searching for something that isn't there. Admit we're husband and wife."

"Very well. You've convinced me that we're married," she conceded. "But that doesn't change the fact that something isn't quite right between us. I suspect a couple can be sexually compatible without being compatible in other ways."

"I'm forced to bow to your superior knowledge," he replied with unmistakable irony. "I have no idea."

She ignored the dig. "You still haven't answered my question. Was I unhappy? Was I planning to leave you?"

"Leave me? Now, why would you think that?"

"Because there must be something," she insisted in frustration. "Some reason to explain—"

"You're chasing shadows."

"Am I?" She searched his face. "Then why did you check me out of the hospital and bring me to this clinic? Explain why I'm not allowed to leave my room unescorted. And tell me why you hired a detective to investigate the crash."

"Where did you hear that?" he demanded.

"Is it true?"

He released her, robbing her of the warmth of his embrace, leaving her strangely bereft. He moved away with lazy grace, a coolness frosting his voice. "Yes. It's true."

"You checked me out of the hospital because some man tried to get in to see me. Who was he?"

Sebastian shrugged. "I don't know. A reporter, I suppose. But I wasn't going to take any chances. I'm a wealthy man. And like it or not, you have to pay the price of that wealth, just as I do. Which means taking advantage of the security this clinic affords and tolerating the occasional escort if I feel the situation warrants it."

"And this situation warrants it?"

"Until you regain your memory...yes."

"Assuming I've actually lost my memory," she reminded dryly. "And the detective?"

"I hired him as a precaution. He'll investigate the crash to make sure nothing is overlooked."

It made perfect sense. She wanted to believe him, to give herself into his care without hesitation or reserve. The attraction between them couldn't be denied. And no matter how hard she fought the certainty that he was her husband, in her heart she knew he'd told her the truth. She felt safe and protected when he held her—and she felt a passion that stunned her, sweeping away every doubt and hesitation.

But something held her back, kept her from making that final commitment. And until she discovered the reason for her misgivings she'd proceed with caution.

"And that's all there is to it?" she asked insistently. "There's nothing more?"

"That's all there is." He thrust a hand through his hair, a weary impatience edging his tone. "Enough, Anna. We've played out this particular game. It's time to end it."

She lifted a skeptical eyebrow. "Have we? Then tell me, Sebastian. If we truly loved each other, how could I forget you?" she asked, bringing into the open the issue that had been bothering her most of all. "How is that possible?"

He turned sharply, the light fading from his eyes, the gray becoming as hard and obdurate as tempered steel. "Perhaps," he stated with cold finality, "you never loved me. Perhaps you found me easy to forget. Whatever the reason, we will get to the truth, you can count on it."

She fought to speak past the thickness blocking her throat. "And how will we do that?"

"By going home, of course."

Home. The word should have brought a sense of reassurance. It didn't. "Home? Where is that?"

"In the Caribbean. To be precise, it's on a small island called *Rochefort* ... Strong Rock."

"*Rochefort*," she repeated, testing the name. "It's not familiar." But then, what was? "When do we leave?"

"Tomorrow. Though the doctors haven't found anything wrong with you, at least nothing definitive, they advise against flying. So, we'll go by boat. It shouldn't take more than a week ..." He shrugged, the movement pulling his shirt taut across his broad chest, sculpting it to the iron-hard muscles beneath. "Four days if weather conditions favor us. That should give you plenty of time to rest and soak up some sun. Who knows. Perhaps by the time you arrive, your memory will have returned."

She gazed at him warily. "And if it has?"

He smiled, though the cool, remote curve of his mouth offered little, if any, reassurance. "Then your homecoming will be extra-special."

Why did that sound so much like a threat? With an urgency born of a sudden, inexplicable apprehension, she scrambled for an alternative. "Can't ... can't we stay here?"

"At the clinic? You're joking."

She suspected he deliberately misunderstood. "In Florida," she clarified tightly. "At least for a while. Perhaps once I've regained my memory we can return home. Do we have family here, anyone who might prompt a memory?"

But he was already shaking his head. "It was one of the things we had in common. Neither of us has any family still living."

"But—"

"There's no point in remaining in Florida," he cut her off. "The doctors advised that the best chance you have of regaining your memory is at home, surrounded by familiar people and places. And that's where I'm taking you." He paused for the space of a heartbeat, before adding with gentle emphasis, "I'm taking you, willing or not."

She caught her breath, a sudden image flashing into her mind—the strange hallucination she'd had while in the hospital. Sebastian stood on the deck of a ship, his feet planted wide, the wind lifting the unruly mane of thick black curls. He held his cutlass half raised, as though ready for action. But it was his expression she remembered most clearly—reckless, passionate, daring... willing to meet any challenge, or overcome any obstacle.

She knew an odd sense of helplessness. Like that buccaneer of old, he'd swept into her life and planned to steal her away. She had no rights, no choice. She was his booty, his plunder, and he intended to take what he wanted.

She drew herself up, searching for the courage she'd decided must be part of her character. "You're taking me, willing or not?" she repeated. "I think you've been living in the Caribbean too long. That sounds like the threat of a pirate."

To her surprise, he grinned, his teeth a flash of white in a bronzed face. And in that instant, he might have been the sea wolf she'd imagined. It disconcerted her, made the resemblance between reality and dreams all the stronger, and all the more difficult to differentiate between. Which was the real man . . . and which the fantasy?

"A pirate?" he repeated, his dark eyebrow winging upward. "You've given yourself away with that one, my love."

She stiffened. "What do you mean?"

"I mean, you're right. I *am* a pirate . . ." His smile faded. "As you damned well know."

CHAPTER THREE

TO ANNA'S dismay, Sebastian left with those words still ringing in her ears. She scarcely heard the arrangements he made to pick her up the next morning. All her focus remained on his statement: "I *am* a pirate... As you damned well know."

What did he mean by that? Was it possible...could he be a *real* pirate? She shook her head. No. The very thought was ludicrous. Fortunately, she wasn't given much time to dwell on it. Throughout the afternoon her various doctors all dutifully trotted through her room, offering platitudes regarding her health, though no iron-clad guarantees.

"Go home and relax," one doctor told her bluntly, while removing the stitches at her temple. "You're wasting your money staying here. There's nothing we can do for you that a little time and rest won't do as well. Probably better."

Throughout the long, endless night, she considered her options, and realized she had only one. For the time being, she'd have to follow where Sebastian led, be his wife in name—and in name only—until her memory returned and she discovered the truth. The truth about her past, her marriage... but especially the truth about her husband.

All too soon morning arrived, and with the coming of the dawn, came Sebastian. He strode into the room, a force as powerful and elemental as nature itself. He'd dressed more casually than she'd ever seen him. Well-worn jeans clung to his hips and muscular thighs. A simple cotton T-shirt outlined every ripple of his chest, the short sleeves stretched by the taut, rounded swell of his biceps. He must have showered right before leaving for the clinic, because his hair was damp, the stubborn curls momentarily subdued.

He held out a small satchel. "I've brought clothes. As soon as you've changed we'll go."

"Thanks," she said, smiling in appreciation. "It'll be good to be dressed again."

She didn't waste any time. Closeting herself in the bathroom, she stripped off her robe and nightgown. After a quick shower, she sorted through the bag, wondering if the sporty white slacks and hot pink tank top she found were her own or more recent purchases. But the moment she put them on, she knew they were hers. She felt at home in the clothes, comfortable, and she sensed the bright, casual outfit matched her personality.

She grinned in relief. Rediscovering herself, she decided, was like constructing a giant jigsaw puzzle without benefit of the finished picture to guide her. Each new piece she fit into the puzzle brought a sense of triumph. And this particular piece told her that despite having a wealthy husband, she didn't feel the need to wear exotic designer fashion, that pleasing colors and comfort were more important than big-name labels. It gave a definite boost to her self-confidence.

Slipping on a pair of canvas deck shoes, she ran a quick brush through her hair, fastening it with a clip so that it fell down her back in an attractive golden-brown stream. After a quick touch-up with the cosmetics she found in the bottom of the tote, she packed up the toiletries cluttering the sink and zipped the satchel closed.

A light knock sounded at the door. "Anna?" Sebastian called. "Are you ready?"

This was it. Time to go. She took a deep breath and glanced in the mirror a final time. How had Sebastian described her? *A proud, stubborn chin. A painful directness lurking about the eyes. An easy smile that suggests a good sense of humor.* Plus courage and self-confidence. She'd need every bit of those qualities to face what lay ahead.

"I'm just finished," she announced, opening the bathroom door. "I think I have everything. A maid came through earlier and packed up all the nightgowns you provided."

"You should have just given them to her."

Startled, her gaze jerked to his. "What do you mean?"

"You know what I mean. You didn't need them before. You won't now."

"You're mistaken," she retorted in clear, precise tones. "I intend to wear each and every one of them."

"Not for long," came his instant retort. "Shall we go?" His hand curved around her arm, his fingers coasting along the soft underside of her arm.

She released her breath in a silent sigh, refusing to dwell on the significance of his suggestive statement. Instead, she took a final look around. It would be good to leave this place. "I'm ready," she said with a nod.

Picking up her bag, he helped her into the wheelchair they still insisted she use and pushed her through the maze of corridors to the front door. For the first time since her injury, she stepped outside, fully clothed

and unfettered. If it weren't for her memory loss, she'd
have felt as free as a bird. She paused, turning her
face skyward. The brilliant sunshine threatened to
scorch her pale skin, but Anna didn't care. The heated
caress felt heavenly. Even the air, weighted with humidity, smelled sweeter than any florist's shop.

She gazed around eagerly, part of her hoping
against hope that something would look familiar... feel familiar. It didn't, and she struggled to
stifle her disappointment. That didn't prove anything, she reassured herself. For all she knew, she'd
never been to this part of Florida before. Besides, she
wouldn't allow anything to destroy her elation at escaping from her bed and from that horrible, pan-
dering clinic. Not her loss of memory... She glanced
at Sebastian.

Not even her concerns about her marriage.

As though sensing her delight at being out of doors,
he didn't hurry. Instead he dropped a protective arm
around her shoulders and strolled with her along the
sidewalk beneath an almost endless row of stubby
windmill palms, their fanlike leaves threatening to snag
in his hair. To her surprise they bypassed the clinic's
parking lot and turned down a residential street.

"I thought you'd appreciate the opportunity to
stretch your legs," he explained in response to her
quizzical glance. "So I parked a little further out."

His consideration warmed her. Had he always been
so thoughtful? Somehow she suspected he had. "I
appreciate that," she said.

She turned her head ever so slightly and watched
him—large, tough, and more handsome than any man
had a right to be. She remembered how he'd been
with her in the bathroom, how he'd brushed her hair.

Her lips twitched in amusement. How he'd helped her put the first pieces of her "personality" jigsaw puzzle together. He might be hard as nails, but it was tempered with an old-world charm and an innate sensuality. Just thinking about being alone with him, knowing his touch... his possession... She shivered, wondering for the umpteenth time how she'd come to marry him—and how she'd manage to stay married to him.

All too soon they reached his car, a sleek black Range Rover. He opened the door for her and helped her climb in. She ran an appreciative hand over the gray leather bucket seats. It looked new and state-of-the-art, containing everything from a cellular phone to a CD player.

"Have I ridden in this car before?" she questioned the moment he slid into the driver's seat.

"Many times."

Her brow crinkled. "I don't remember. I keep waiting for something... anything to feel the least bit familiar. But it never does."

He started to say something, then changed his mind at the last minute. "Fasten your seat belt," he requested, and started the engine.

She complied, shooting him a troubled look. "Wasn't I wearing one when...?" She couldn't finish the question, flinching from the mere suggestion.

"Yes, you were." He turned the key, the Range Rover coming to life with a muted roar. "According to the rescue crew, it saved your life."

It took her a moment to absorb that, to rally enough to ask her next question. "Was I driving?"

He shifted into reverse and eased from the parking spot. A moment later they shot down the wide, residential street. "You were alone in the car when you were found." He lifted an eyebrow. "Why the questions all of the sudden? You never bothered to ask about this at the clinic."

She shrugged. "It's only just occurred to me. I guess I didn't want to know before. Tell me what happened. Did I drive off the road?" She caught her breath, turning sharply to face him. "I didn't hit anyone, did I?"

He spared her a brief glance. "Relax. Yours was the only vehicle involved."

"Then tell me what happened," she repeated.

He took his time replying, as though considering how much he wanted to say. "It was raining. The roads were slick. The car took a curve at too high a speed and didn't make it. End of story."

But it wasn't. She couldn't shake the overwhelming impression that he kept some vital detail from her. "The *car* took the curve at too high a speed or *I* did?" He didn't respond, the grim set of his mouth warning that he had no intention of answering. Not that it mattered. If she were the only occupant of the car, she'd been at fault, driving recklessly on roads too slippery for such high speeds. She tried a different tack. "Where were you?"

"At a nearby hotel. We'd come to Florida on business."

That caught her by surprise. "What sort of business?"

"I design small private aircraft. One of my planes was ready to go into production. It was important I be here in case we hit any snags."

She nodded, a thousand questions about his business flooding her mind. But for the time being it seemed more important to focus on the accident. "And I left the hotel to run some errands, or something?"

"It's possible. You didn't tell me your plans. The police arrived at the hotel to inform me of the accident."

Her brows drew together in confusion. "They knew how to get in touch with you?"

"The police called the factory, figuring the management would have my number."

"The factory where they were constructing your airplane?" He nodded, confirming her guess. It gave her pause. If that were true, it meant the authorities had been able to make a connection between whatever identification she'd carried and Sebastian, and then connect Sebastian's name with the factory. It didn't take long for the full implication to sink in. "You're that well-known?"

"Yes."

No hesitation, no equivocation. Just a flat, cool confirmation. No wonder he'd been so impatient with her doubts about their marriage. Rich, famous... She peeked at him from beneath her lashes. Or more likely *infamous*. So much for her fears he might be a real, live pirate. She frowned, troubled by one rather significant detail. If he were that renowned, what in the world had he seen in her? How had she managed to catch the eye of someone like Sebastian Kane?

The questions poured out, fast and furious. "How did we meet?"

"You worked for me."

"And we fell in love. Just like that?"

"I'd say that about sums it up."

"Did we know each other for long before we married?"

"About six months."

She turned to study him. "That's hardly any time at all," she observed.

"Now that's one of the few things you've said that I agree with." A wry smile touched his mouth. "Any more questions?"

"Just one... Who's Chris?" she asked impulsively.

He stopped at a light and glanced at her, his expression calm, yet utterly unreadable. "You look like hell. Are you worrying again?"

"Still."

He reached out and punched the power button for the CD player. Instantly the opening strains of Andrew Lloyd Webber's, *The Phantom of the Opera* filled the Range Rover. "You always claimed it was one of your favorites," he said. "Maybe it will help you relax."

"You still haven't answered my question," she reminded, refusing to be distracted.

"Sorry," came the dry retort. The light turned and he eased out the clutch, accelerating through the intersection. "I was more concerned with your well-being."

"I appreciate that, but I'd like to know who Chris is." She didn't know why she chose that moment to ask. She'd just suddenly recalled her initial conversation with Sebastian when she'd awakened...and his resulting anger. Considering his current reaction, he'd have preferred not to answer. "The first day, when I regained consciousness," she prompted. "You asked me who he was."

He nodded. "I remember. You spoke his name when I arrived at the hospital. I don't know why. Nor do I know who he is." His expression might have been carved from stone. He stared straight ahead, emotionless and remote. "I guess we won't find out until you regain your memory."

"Then why—"

He exhaled sharply. "Leave it alone, Anna. Put your head back, close your eyes and relax. We still have an hour's drive ahead of us."

"But, I have more questions."

"And I'll answer them. We'll have all the time in the world once we get to the boat. Give it a rest for now." He glanced at her, and she saw the flash of concern beneath the dispassionate exterior. "Don't run before you can walk, Anna. You'll only get frustrated."

As much as she hated to admit it, he offered sound advice. The questions bubbled through her mind like a pot on the stove with the heat turned on too high. And the few answers she'd received only made the situation worse, increasing her turmoil. With a sigh, she leaned her head back and closed her eyes, focusing on the haunting music. Sebastian was right. No matter how many times she listened to it, *Phantom* had never yet failed to sweep her away, carrying her into a delightful realm of fantasy and magic.

Her lashes flickered, a pinprick of awareness disturbing the smooth tenor of her thoughts, a realization that something notable had occurred. But whatever it was slipped from her subconscious before she could fully grasp its significance. She stifled a yawn. She was tired. Very tired. A restless night worrying about returning "home" combined with several days' worth of stress caught up with her and sleep finally claimed her.

She dreamt.

Like some spectral observer she was aware of that fact, but couldn't seem to force herself awake, nor escape the darkness of the dream. She rode in a car, arguing heatedly with someone. But she couldn't hear the words, nor see whom she spoke to. She turned her head to look at her companion, an angry response on her lips, despair in her heart. When she looked back out the windshield, the total darkness disoriented her. And then the sky lit up and she realized too late that the road ahead turned.

"Look out!" she shrieked, coming bolt upright.

The Range Rover swerved violently, then skidded to a halt on the shoulder of the road. "What the *hell* is the matter with you?" Sebastian bit out. "Why did you scream like that?"

"I'm sorry! I didn't mean to." Anna covered her face, her hands trembling uncontrollably. To her utter humiliation, she burst into tears. "I saw something," she managed to say through the sobs choking her.

With a soft curse, he thrust open his door and exited, circling the vehicle to the passenger side. In a matter of seconds he had her free of her seat and wrapped in his arms. He held her for several long minutes, letting her cry it out.

He waited until her tears had abated somewhat before complaining gently, "You're getting my shirt wet."

"I'm... I'm sorry," she said again, pulling back and brushing at the damp stain on the shoulder of his cotton T-shirt. Not that it did any good.

"Don't be sorry," he ordered with a tenderness she couldn't mistake. His knuckle slipped beneath her chin and he tilted her face upward, gazing down at her in concern. "What happened?"

"I'm not sure. I was dreaming. I think I remembered the accident." She shook her head in confusion. "I don't know. It's all a jumble."

"Do you think being in a car again precipitated it?"

She released an exhausted sigh. "It's possible."

"Can you remember any of the dream?"

"I think so," she said with a nod, struggling to summon the disjointed images. Only still-frame flashes remained, hazy bits and pieces that were vanishing as quickly as wisps of fog beneath a midday sun. She grappled to hold on to the memories before they disappeared.

"You were in the car..." he prompted.

"I think I was angry." She made the confession in a low, distressed voice. "But I'm not certain why. I remember looking out of the windshield and realizing everything was pitch black, like someone had turned out the lights. Then the sky lit up and I saw that the road ahead curved and...and..." She shook her head, unable to continue.

To her relief, he didn't press. He pulled her close, holding her within the hard, protective strength of his arms. "It's okay, Anna. Let it go," he murmured.

"I wish I could," she said, choking on the words. "I...I keep seeing the very end, when the car left the road surface. I covered my face with my hands." She caught her breath in a gasp. Pulling back, she stared up at him in horror. "I covered my face! I shouldn't have done that. I should have kept holding on to the steering wheel. But..." Her brows pulled together in a frown, the fragments of memory at odds with what she knew must have happened. "Somehow I couldn't. Maybe if I'd kept steering—if I hadn't let go . . ."

"Instinct took over." His fingers feathered across the small, angry scar at her temple. "If you hadn't protected your face, this could have been far worse."

"But—"

He shook his head, his hand moving to her mouth, halting the words before they could be uttered. "Stop judging yourself, Anna. In an emergency situation, you react first. Later is the time for regrets and recriminations and second guesses. And by then they're pointless. What happened, happened. It's done. Let it go."

She nodded. He was right. She couldn't change the past, not even with all the remorse in the world. She clung to the knowledge, drawing what cold comfort she could from it. "This is good, isn't it?" she offered with a shaky smile. "Perhaps my memory is returning."

"Looks like it." He glanced at the Range Rover. "We can't stay here any longer. It isn't safe. Can you handle getting back in the car?"

Her laugh sounded watery. "Without falling to pieces, you mean? I think so." She eyed the vehicle apprehensively. "Not that there's much choice. I guess walking isn't a viable option."

"No," he agreed. "I'd rather not, if it's all the same to you."

She drew in a deep breath. "I can do it." Sure she could. *Maybe*.

"Okay. We'll take it slow and easy. There's no rush."

She hesitated outside the gaping door. "Do you mind if I don't nap anymore?"

An odd tightness swept across his face, an expression she could have sworn was contrition deepening the lines bracketing his mouth. "That should have occurred to me. I'm sorry."

"You weren't to know," she said, letting him off the hook. Once more she glanced at the Range Rover, dreading the prospect of returning to the vehicle. Without giving herself time to reconsider, she climbed in and fastened her seat belt. "Let's go," she told him in a taut little voice.

He didn't give her a chance to change her mind. He slammed the door closed and within seconds had the car started and in motion. He glanced at her once and frowned, that one, brief look speaking volumes. Did she look as fragile as she felt? Determined to erase all traces of tears, she reached in the back for her tote, removing the bag of cosmetics.

No wonder he'd frowned, she decided, peering into a compact mirror. Her eyes looked bruised and vulnerable, her complexion pale and drawn. Even her mouth was set in a tense, rigid line. She set about correcting what she could, knowing that nothing could alter the touch of fear lingering in her golden-brown eyes. The dream had terrified her, the aftereffects haunting, refusing to go away.

To her relief, they arrived at a pretty little harbor just as she capped her lipstick. Sebastian parked in a small lot reserved for long-term parking and, grabbing her tote from the back, guided her along the quay. Sailboats filled the slips, their masts swaying in a gentle dance that matched the metallic clanging of the rigging. The sun spilled down on them, hot and radiant, making Anna grateful for the cooling breeze,

even though it carried the unmistakable scent of salt
and fish and the faintly sour odor of diesel fuel.

"Through here," Sebastian said, unlocking a gate
that lead onto a private dock.

She stopped dead, indicated the sleek powerboat
secured to the cleats a few feet away. "We're going
to your island in that? Looks like fun, but sleeping
may be a problem."

An odd smile touched his mouth. "No. We're going
in *that*."

She looked where he pointed and froze, her brows
pulling together. *That* was a huge boat anchored off-
shore. No. Not a boat. More like a ship. The QE III,
perhaps? "You own it?" she questioned in disbelief,
knowing before he responded what his answer would
be.

"Yes."

She shook her head. "No. No way."

"What's wrong now?"

How could she explain? How could she possibly
put into words what she felt? She didn't belong to this
world. She knew it with an instinctive certainty.
Nothing about this situation was the least bit familiar
or comfortable. Not the powerful black motorboat,
not the huge gleaming ship—and especially not the
formidable man at her side. The uneven planking
shifted beneath her feet, rising and dipping with the
gentle roll of the tidal flow.

She turned on him.

"It was late, the night of the accident," she said,
speaking fast, her voice low and strained. "Well past
dark. And there was a storm, wasn't there?" She
paused, waiting to see if he offered a response. If his
fingers hadn't clenched around the leather handles of

her tote in a white-knuckle grip, she'd have thought her revelations hadn't made any impression at all. "I'm right, aren't I?"

"Yes."

It didn't make sense that he'd keep the information from her. There had to be a logical explanation. "Why didn't you tell me?"

"I did." His glance swept over her, a fleeting, silvery-gray flash, cool and analytical and frighteningly remote. "I told you it was raining."

She shook her head. "In the dream ... That wasn't just a rain shower, it was a storm. The rain came down so hard I couldn't see the road ahead. Then the lightning cut the dark, blinding in its intensity, and the road seemed to vanish before my eyes ..." Her voice faltered, before gaining renewed strength. "Why didn't you tell me?" she repeated the demand.

He stared out across the harbor. "It's important you recall the details on your own."

Anger simmered. "Why? What possible difference would it make?"

At last he focused on her. "That way the memories are real. They aren't planted there by me, born from desperation instead of from reality."

"Is that your opinion or some of the clinic psychologist's mumbo jumbo?"

His mouth firmed. "It worked, didn't it? I didn't tell you about the storm, or that it was night."

"Or why I was out so late, in such adverse conditions." She folded her arms across her chest, her eyes narrow and watchful. "Why would I do something so foolish?"

"I don't know."

"Don't you?" The question hung between them for an endless moment. "Or is it that you *won't* tell me?"

"We're wasting time, Anna. Get in the boat."

She took a hasty step backward. "Not yet. Not until we have this out."

He stiffened, as though holding himself in check, as though fighting the urge to grab her and force her to his will. "Then I suggest you get to the point. Because we're leaving in five minutes."

She inclined her head. "Very well. The point is... I don't trust you. You expect me to go with you, do what you say, *believe* what you say." She shrugged helplessly. "But how can I do that when you're not being honest with me?"

A muscle leapt in his jaw. "I'm not being honest? Coming from you, that's almost funny."

"I'm dead serious. You're keeping secrets. *Why*?"

He took a step closer and for the first time she saw the pain and urgency simmering beneath his iron control. And she saw something else. A fierce, over-riding determination. "If there are any secrets between us, they're locked away where I can't get at them. Locked in the past—a past you claim you don't remember."

She stared at him, stunned. "You expect me to believe that?"

He shrugged. "That's up to you. Believe what I tell you or don't, it's your choice. But in time, a memory will come back, just as it did today in the car. And when it does, I'll be there. And then we'll both know the truth."

She remained silent for a long moment, gazing down at the rough wooden planks of the pier, digesting his remarks. Finally, she looked at him. "Tell me, Sebastian. Is that how our sea trip to your home is going to be? You constantly watching me, feeding me bits and pieces of my past while you wait to see if I remember . . . ready to pounce if I inadvertently discover what's really wrong between us."

"What are you talking about?"

"I'm not stupid. I know there's something very wrong with our relationship. And it has to do with that night, doesn't it?"

Without a word, he turned and strode to the end of the dock. After a moment's hesitation, she followed. Tossing her satchel into the boat, he turned and faced her. "I'll tell you this one last time. I don't know why you went out that night. I wish to God I did. But you didn't bother to inform me. When you regain your memory, we'll discuss this further. Until then, I have nothing more to say."

She lifted her chin. "And if I insist on discussing it now?"

"Then you'll be talking to thin air." He thrust a hand through his hair, an edge of impatience coloring his voice. "What's the problem? Why are you pushing this? Once on board you'll have time to relax, enjoy the sea and salt air. And maybe then, you'll remember."

"I'm not a fool, Sebastian," came her instant retort. "I know why you're so desperate to get me on that boat and to your island."

He stilled. "And why is that?"

"Because you'll have me on your home turf, beneath your control." The whisper came from the heart, desperate in its appeal. "I need time. I need space. I can't relax with you constantly on guard, watching everything I do, analyzing every word I utter.''

"I'm not leaving you." He reached for her, grasping her shoulders, his hands warm against the bared skin at her neckline. "We're going to *Rochefort*, you and I, whether you're willing or not."

"I'll go. And on your boat, if you insist," she attempted to compromise. "But I want to make the trip alone."

"Not a chance. I won't leave you unprotected."

"Why not?" The words burst from her. "What could happen to me? I'm trapped on a boat in the middle of the Caribbean." She glanced at the huge waiting vessel, shivering apprehensively. "You must have a dozen crew members aboard that thing. I'm sure they'll keep me safe."

"I don't pay my crew to be watchdogs. Nor do I relish having to fire any of them."

Her gaze flew to his. "Fire them? What are you talking about?"

His hands tightened, his thumbs sweeping across the fragile bones at the joining of her neck and shoulders. "If anything went wrong, I'd fire the man responsible."

She shook her head, appalled. "No. That's not fair. You wouldn't—"

"I would," he stated unequivocally. "And I'd do it without compunction. I won't have you at risk, nor allow anyone's carelessness to put you at risk. You have no memory, no money and for some reason you're beginning to feel desperate. And desperate people are notorious for making bad decisions."

"You make me sound like a child!" she protested.

"Until you regain your memory you're as defenseless as one." He drew her closer, overriding her attempts to pull away with infuriating ease. "Anna, I know I'm asking a lot. But you have to trust me. I swear on everything I hold dear, I'd never do anything to hurt you."

"Then why won't you tell me the truth?" she cried.

He didn't release her, though his grasp gentled. "The truth is something we'll have to discover together. Come with me, sweetheart," he urged with infinite tenderness. "Don't fight me over this. You'll only wear yourself out resisting the inevitable."

"Resisting the inevitable? You mean resist being abducted by a pirate," she shot back.

"Abducted?" He had the audacity to laugh. "If this were another century, you might be right. I'd sweep down on you in my schooner and steal you away to my tropical island."

"Isn't that what you're doing now?"

He cocked his head to one side. "Does it appeal to the romantic in you? Shall I indulge your fantasies?"

"No!"

Before she could ward him off, he swept her into his arms. With a dangerous smile, he leapt with catlike grace into the boat, depositing her stunned and breathless into the passenger seat. Her heart raced, her body felt hot and aroused, her senses quivering with life as though absorbing every scent, every sight and sound, every nuance to be had from those brief moments in his arms.

"Consider yourself my captive," he informed her with a lazy grin.

He stood above her, tall and indomitable, more in his element than she'd ever seen him. His black hair reflected the rays of strong, golden sunshine and his eyes flashed with the same silver glitter as the fingerlings that schooled just beneath the surface of the jewel-blue water. He belonged to the sea, she realized then. He commanded that same leashed power, the same ability to stir to life with monumental passion and strength, lashing any who were foolish enough to underestimate him.

The powerful engine of the motorboat throbbed to life and he cast off from the dock, pointing the prow toward the yacht. She glanced back at the shore, watching as they drew further and further away. Sebastian shifted closer, catching a fistful of her hair, allowing the wind to sweep it through his fingers in a cascade of gleaming golds and browns.

"Don't look back," he ordered. "There's nothing there for you. It's time to look ahead."

"I'm not sure I want to look ahead," she confessed.

His gaze locked with hers and for a brief moment a hint of compassion touched his expression before it hardened, settling in resolute lines. "You don't have any choice, my love. That's the only direction available to us."

CHAPTER FOUR

To ANNA'S surprise she fell in love with the boat, finding the subtle blend of old and new of immense appeal—the old wood and classic design balanced with a modern sophistication and elegance. Sebastian gave her an abbreviated tour of the vessel, leaving her to freshen up in an impressively large suite and requesting she join him on deck as soon as convenient.

She didn't waste any time, the warm sun and balmy breezes were all the inducement she needed to return to the deck. But before she left the cabin, she shot a quick, troubled glance toward the spacious bed—the mattress more than ample for two. Was this his subtle way of letting her know they'd be sharing the suite— and the bed? If so, he'd soon learn differently. Until she regained her memory, she had no intention of permitting any intimacies. No matter what it took, she'd find a way to hold him at a distance.

She sank onto the bed with a sigh of defeat.

Right. Just look at how successful she'd been yesterday in the arboretum. One touch and she lost all ability to think, every sense coming alive beneath his hands and lips. Well, she'd have to find a way to avoid those hands and lips...and more importantly, to avoid his mind-splintering kisses. She shivered, leaping from the bed as though it were a deadly snare set to entrap her. If only she didn't find those kisses so utterly, undeniably delicious.

As soon as she returned to the deck, she realized something was very wrong. Sebastian stared down at a piece of paper—clearly a message of some sort—and conferred with a steward in low tones. At her approach, he stuffed the missive in his pocket and dismissed the crewman.

"It seems you'll have your way, after all," he informed her, his eyes turning a dark, pewter gray.

She gazed at him in bewilderment. "I don't understand. Is something wrong?"

"A small problem, but one I'm forced to deal with in person. I'll be leaving in a few minutes."

"Leaving the boat?" At his nod, she asked, "Do I go with you or stay here?"

He didn't hesitate. "You stay. I've instructed the captain to put out to sea as soon as I've disembarked."

"We're going on without you."

It wasn't a question, but a statement of fact. He really intended to leave her, she realized with dawning dismay. She should be thrilled. For some inexplicable reason, she wasn't. Since she'd first opened her eyes in the hospital, the one constant in her life had been Sebastian. Now that was about to change. He would be gone and she'd be left in the care of complete strangers.

He reached out, snagging her chin with the knuckle of his index finger. "Try and control your disappointment, my love," he said in a dry voice, misreading her reaction. "I'll see if I can't clear up this matter and join you somewhere *en route*."

She smiled sweetly, relieved that for once she'd managed to keep her thoughts private. "Please don't rush on my account," she informed him with deceptive composure. "Feel free to take your time."

His bark of laughter caught her by surprise. "You're consistent, I'll give you that much."

"You'd do well to remember it."

"And you'd do well to remember this."

Without warning he grasped her arms and tugged her close, quelling her instinctive resistance. His hands were warm and heavy through her cotton tank top, his fingers painting lazy circles along her shoulders. With nerve-racking frequency he encroached past the edge of her neckline, caressing the sensitive hollows of her collarbone and stealing up along the side of her throat to the hot, throbbing pulse beneath her jaw.

Color blossomed in her cheeks and a tiny, helpless groan escaped before she could suppress it. She held very, very still, struggling to distance herself from his touch, his scent, the mesmerizing murmur of his voice. But she could no more prevent the small, agitated tremor of longing, a tremor that shook her to the very core, than she could prevent the relentless surge of the ocean beneath her. She prayed he wouldn't notice the flood of heat suffusing her body, or the frantic rush of her breath—desperate to believe he couldn't detect the sweet warmth gathering in her loins.

But he saw, she quickly realized. He saw all that, and far more. He was too sophisticated to remain unaware, too acutely tuned to a woman's needs and to the subtle clues that bared her most secret desires.

Oh, yes. He knew.

"You want me, Anna," he murmured, confirming her worst fears. "Every time I touch you, I can feel it, sense it."

She shook her head in useless denial. "You're wrong."

"Am I? Let's see."

He slid a hand into her hair, releasing the clip. It clattered to the teak deck, a splash of vivid pink against the warm, polished wood. The wind lifted her hair, tossing the golden-brown strands across her cheek. He swept them back, following the line of her jaw with his thumb, his hand cradling the nape of her neck and tilting up her head.

She couldn't move, could scarcely breathe. How was it possible that he could so easily mesmerize her, that with one touch, one glance from those turbulent gray eyes she would melt against him, lift her face and accept the possession of his mouth?

And his kiss was a possession. He took, his lips hard and demanding, storming her defenses, breaching her barriers to seek the sweet honey within. There was no retreat, only surrender. She moaned, a soft, wild whisper of yearning that caused his body to harden against hers, encouraged him to slide his hands the length of her spine and cup her bottom, locking her snug within his lean hips.

"The crew," she protested, gasping for air, her lungs filled with the subtle, male scent of him. He smelled of wind and sea and salt, tantalizing and unique . . . and oddly arousing.

"The crew is too well-trained to interrupt." He stared down at her, his eyes the color of smoke, his gaze burning like a white-hot flame. "Besides, the overhang hides us from any curious eyes."

"I know what you're doing," she told him, struggling for control. "And it won't work."

He tilted his head to one side in an endearingly familiar gesture. "What won't work?"

"I won't be seduced by you. Not until I have my memory back."

A slow smile crept across his mouth. "Perhaps if I seduce you, it will give you the one thing you want most. I know it will give me what I want most."

"And what's that?" she dared to ask.

"My wife." He rested his hands on the feminine flare of her hips, holding her tight against him, his thumbs drifting beneath her shirt and across the taut planes of her belly in a seductive caress. "It will give me back my wife."

She trembled at his words, not doubting for a minute that fervent desire marked her face, an unmistakable hunger only he could sate. He continued to stroke, his fingers inching upward to follow the gentle curve of her ribs, pausing for a heart-stopping moment beneath the ripe fullness of her breasts. He didn't move, didn't encroach further. They stood frozen, and those few, impossibly tense seconds seemed to last an eternity. Then he flattened his palms, his nails grazing the silk-covered underside of her breasts.

She nearly came unhinged.

Covering his hands with hers, she shook her head, the violent movement tangling her loose hair about her neck and shoulders. She didn't trust herself enough to speak, reluctant to fight him verbally, afraid of giving herself away. Not that she hadn't already, damn him!

"No?" he questioned, his voice a husky rumble.

"No!" Her reply was more gasp than word.

"Then the least you can do is offer me a farewell kiss."

She struggled for control, fought to hide the extent of his power over her emotions. She licked her lips, her tongue probing the swollen fullness of her mouth.

"You've had that already," she protested. "And then some."

"I was forced to take a kiss. Now I want one in return, one freely given." He lifted an eyebrow. "Is that too much to ask of my wife?"

"Too much to ask? When has that ever stopped you?" she demanded, the questions swift and distressed.

"Don't," he murmured, and for a crazy instant she could have sworn he spoke tenderly. "A simple salute of farewell. That's all I'm asking."

"Take your hands off me first."

His hold tightened. "Hands are a necessary component of a kiss. Or have you forgotten?"

"I haven't forgotten how to kiss," she retorted sharply. "I've only forgotten you." The lines bracketing his mouth deepened and she felt a sudden compunction, but she didn't dare soften, to allow him to appeal to any gentler, more vulnerable feelings she might possess. It would be too dangerous. It would court disaster. "Since this is to be my kiss, we do it my way," she finished. "So take your hands off me."

She didn't think he'd do it. Then with a slow, knowing smile, his hands shifted, the leisurely exploration back down her ribs and across her abdomen an insidious torture. Her muscles tightened reflexively, her breath catching in her throat as she battled for rational thought. His grip halted at her hips for an endless moment, forcefully tight and filled with intense male aggression. Just when she thought she'd reached the breaking point, he dropped his hands to his sides.

"Anything else you want from me?" he asked with deceptive calm.

"You aren't to touch me—"

He lifted an eyebrow. "No touching? A kiss does involve a certain amount of touching. Or is that something else that's slipped your mind?"

"I haven't forgotten that, either," she snapped. "You know what I mean! Keep your hands to yourself. No grabbing, groping or...or... You know!"

He crowded her back against the wall beneath the overhang. "No 'you know'? None at all? Not even, say, this...?"

The breath exploded from her lungs and she closed her eyes, caught between the ship's cool, unyielding wall and the equally unyielding heat of an aroused male body. She knew, with a certainty that defied understanding, that if he continued to press himself against her in such a graphic, intimate way, she'd surrender everything to him. And if that happened, she'd lose all hope of retaining the tattered shreds of her dignity...of preserving her self-respect.

"*Bastian!*" His name left her lips in a frantic plea. Immediately, he stepped back, an odd, searching expression on his face. She could have wept in relief despite the fact that he'd left her weak-kneed and trembling. If it weren't for the wall supporting her, she questioned whether she'd even be able to remain upright. "Please. No more."

"Very well," he said, a satisfied smile easing the tense lines of his mouth. "No more...'you know.'"

She dragged air into her lungs, shooting him a fulminating glare. "That was low, even for you."

"You still owe me a kiss."

She considered protesting, but suspected if she didn't agree, he'd take by force what she refused to surrender willingly. "Are you going to behave?" she questioned, her dark eyes wary.

"I'll try."

She wouldn't win any further concessions from him, and to delay any longer would only invite trouble. Not giving herself time to reconsider, she took the two steps necessary to bring her within kissing range. Circling his neck with her arms, she gazed up at him.

"One kiss, freely given as ordered," she said softly.

Nothing before that moment had seemed the least familiar. Not Sebastian, not even his embraces, despite the ardent responses he'd managed to wring from her. And yet, in the most natural of movements, as though she'd done it countless· times before, she tilted her head a mere fraction and covered his mouth with hers in the sweetest of kisses.

He didn't grab her, didn't sweep her into his arms. If she hadn't known better, she'd almost suspect he feared touching her, feared ending such a tender moment. His lips were firm and wide and her mouth shifted ever so slightly over his, tasting him, aware that his lips had parted, inviting a more thorough exploration. But she didn't take advantage of the offer, shying away from the deeper intimacy.

And yet...

She was tempted. If the circumstances had been different, if she weren't so certain that Sebastian was motivated by a desire to reestablish their marital bonds before her memory returned, if he were less intimidating, less potently male, she might have thrown caution to the winds. Instead, she took her time, nibbled lightly, lingering where she willed before ending the kiss. Her lips seeming to cling to his for a final instant, as though reluctant to bring the interlude to a close. And then, she slid her arms from around his neck and stepped away from him, surprisingly shaken considering the gentle nature of the embrace.

"You're trembling," he observed. "I wonder why."

"The wind is chilly," she murmured, her gaze slipping from his.

His quiet laugh brought a flush to her cheeks. "Try again."

"You know why I'm trembling," she informed him gravely, holding on to her composure through sheer willpower. She could only hope that blatant honesty— as stark and painful as it was—would end his taunting.

But he gave no quarter. "Tell me. Admit the truth. Say it out loud. Now. Before I leave."

Stubbornly, she shook her head, unwilling to relent, refusing to hand him so much power. "There's nothing to admit."

"You continue to deny what you feel...to deny us. *Why?*"

"Because I don't trust you." She barely murmured her response, but he heard, heard and drew back, his expression growing cool and shuttered.

"That makes two of us," he said.

She glanced at him. "A stalemate, Sebastian?"

"For the moment," he conceded. "But only until you arrive at *Rochefort*."

She folded her arms across her chest. "Don't count on it. Until my memory clears and I remember what's wrong between us—and I know there's something wrong, despite your denials—I prefer to keep my distance."

"You play this game very well, Anna," came his cryptic reply. "But you won't win. You'll slip up. And when you do, I'll have the truth from you."

She stirred nervously. "Why does that sound like a threat?"

"Because it is," he stated with a directness that stunned her. "But until then, there's one final detail to take care of." He thrust his hand into his pocket and pulled out a small jeweler's box, flipping it open with his thumb. "Your wedding rings."

Anna stared at the bands tucked into the folds of white velvet, the blood draining from her face. One was a platinum ring guard, encircled with diamonds. The other was a simple solitaire, large and square, in a beautiful, old-fashioned setting. The diamonds caught the sunlight, shooting off sparks of multi-colored fire. Time froze and in her mind's eye, she saw those very same rings. Only the light catching in the diamonds was different—harsher, whiter, striking off them as they tumbled over and over through the air.

"Anna?"

She dragged her gaze from the mesmerizing sparkle, struggling to free herself from the painful flash of memory. "Where...where did those come from?" she whispered.

"I gave them to you. On our wedding day." His eyes narrowed. "Do you remember them? Do they mean something to you?"

She backed away, holding up a hand. "Please. Keep them. I'll...I'll wear them when I get to your island."

"Oh, no, my sweet." He caught her hand in his. Removing the rings from the box, he slipped them onto her finger. They fit perfectly. "They stay there, do you understand?'' he insisted, as though suspecting she'd remove them the instant he left.

''Why?'' she cried, stepping free of his hold. ''What difference can it possibly make? Either we're married or we're not.'' She stared at her hand, catching her lip between her teeth. ''This doesn't change a thing.''

''In the hospital, you said we couldn't be married because you wore no rings, because there wasn't a mark on your finger to indicate you'd ever worn them. Well, the rings are now on your hand. And, by heaven, there will be a mark on your finger by the time you reach *Rochefort*.''

She lifted her chin. ''And if there isn't?''

''There will be,'' he said, refusing to back down. ''I hope we understand each other.''

He didn't wait for her response, but turned and left . . . left her standing there, the rings on her hand an almost unbearable weight.

Anna decided not to tell Sebastian about the nightmares. They started her first night at sea, brief flashes of the accident played out in non-ending, slow-motion dreams. Sleeping became an ordeal, something she avoided, and she soon saw the detrimental results in the full-length mirror in her cabin. She lost weight she could ill afford to lose. Hollows appeared beneath her cheekbones and purple bruises shadowed her eyes. Even with the tan she slowly acquired, she looked drawn and wan.

She quickly discovered that the only surcease from the nightmares were the times she drifted off in the lounger on deck. There, beneath the steamy warmth and sultry tropic breezes she could sleep without fear, her dreams filled instead with images of Sebastian—

his deep, husky voice, his passionate kisses, the power of his arms as they held her tight against his chest. And each time she dreamt of him, she'd wake with his name on her lips, plagued by an odd restlessness that lasted for hours.

The days passed and Sebastian continued to be delayed by business obligations. Relief vied with disappointment. Relief that she didn't have to endure any more of their confrontations; a confusing disappointment that she could no longer count on his strength and support. And to her dismay, a tiny, traitorous part of her suspected that if he'd been with her in that huge, lonely bed, perhaps the nightmares wouldn't have been so horrifying, perhaps his presence would have held them at bay.

Certainly without him they came as regular as clockwork.

The next four days blended one into another, the intense sun and incredible blue ocean a constant delight. She was surprised to find a closet full of clothing in the cabin—gorgeous dresses, skirts and blouses, all a perfect fit and unquestionably her own. The built-in dresser drawers were filled with silken undergarments and every accessory she could ever use. And to her relief, she discovered that the bathing suits she unearthed were modest, one-piece affairs with matching wraps, nothing to shock or dismay or that she considered too risqué to wear in front of the crew.

It should have been perfect.

For some reason, it wasn't.

With a sigh, she rolled onto her back, adjusting her hat and sunglasses to keep the intense sunshine off her face. She reached for the tumbler of freshly squeezed orange juice resting on the table at her elbow and she took a quick, restorative sip. Why couldn't she relax? Why, with each passing day, did she grow more and more tense, like a clockwork spring coiling tighter and tighter?

She sat up, drawing her knees to her chest. She couldn't avoid the truth any longer...that her tension was directly linked to Sebastian. That with each day that passed without his return, her apprehension increased, along with an exhausting combination of nervousness and excitement as she waited to see if *this* would be the day he came to her.

"Excuse me, Mrs. Kane."

A crewman approached, and she waited anxiously to hear what he had to tell her. She'd soon discovered the only time they disturbed her was if they had a message from Sebastian. "Yes, Josie. What is it?"

The crewman touched his cap with a thumb and forefinger. "The captain wanted you to know that we're approaching *Rochefort*."

She stiffened. "So soon?"

"We made better time than expected. The island is off the starboard bow, if you're interested."

"Thank you." She stood, gathering her belongings. "I'll go change and then have a look."

For reasons she didn't care to analyze, she took her time dressing, selecting a split skirt in a cheerful red floral print and a thin cotton blouse. She styled her hair in a tidy French braid and applied makeup, using a heavy hand with both the concealer and blush. She gazed at her reflection, praying she'd successfully hidden the strain she'd been under. Though knowing Sebastian's hawklike scrutiny, she somehow doubted it.

Deciding she'd done the best she could with her appearance, she returned to the deck, standing at the rail and staring in equal parts wonder and alarm at the dark rocky island they rapidly approached. It thrust out of the sea, an odd mist clinging to the upper peaks and along the convoluted folds of the landscape. As they motored closer the lushness of the forest became more apparent, the mountainside seeming to rise straight up out of the heaving ocean, without beach or break. It looked hard and secluded and untamed.

Like Sebastian.

A glint of metal caught her eye and a lethal-looking speedboat appeared on the horizon, rocketing across the water toward them. She knew it was Sebastian. Even before he came close enough to recognize, something about his autocratic bearing and the absolute control with which he handled the boat warned that it would be him. Her heart began to pound, the blood rushing through her veins as fast as his speedboat flew across the waves. Her fingers curled around the rail, her palms slick with nervous perspiration.

Easing in close to the yacht, he lifted a hand in greeting, his dark hair glinting beneath the golden sun like a raven's wings. "Care to jump?" he called up to her with a wicked grin.

She shook her head. "No, thanks."

"Do you think you can climb down the ladder? I'll catch you if you fall."

She hesitated, then nodded, waiting for a crewman to assist her. It seemed an impossibly long way. But she knew Sebastian would keep her safe. She didn't question how she knew, refused to consider the implications of that knowledge. She just climbed down, rung by rung until he fastened strong hands about her waist.

"Miss me?" he asked.

She tumbled into his arms, clinging to him as though he were her sole lifeline. Before she had time to catch her breath, let alone formulate a response, he kissed her. A hot, passionate, fierce kiss that seared her mouth and wiped every thought from her head. She clutched at his shirt, wishing she could blame her loss of equilibrium on the restless movement of the ocean beneath her feet. But her reaction had far more to do with the man who held her than to the choppy roll of the seas.

"You're here," she said, the inane words coming out in breathless confusion. "I...I wasn't sure you would be."

He searched her face, his gaze probing. "I wasn't about to miss your homecoming." A frown pulled his dark brows together. "I thought you were supposed to relax. What have you been doing to yourself? You look like hell."

"Thanks a lot!" She pulled free of his embrace. Slipping into the passenger seat, she fixed her attention on the island.

"I'm concerned, Anna," he informed her in clipped tones. "And with good cause. I expected you to look rested."

She wrapped her arms about her waist, unable to meet his penetrating stare. How could she defend herself when he stated the truth? Besides, he hadn't said anything she didn't already know. Her appearance *had* suffered. She just didn't want him to find out why—didn't want to explain about the nightmares.

"It's hard to relax when everything is so uncertain," she finally said.

"Your memory...?"

Unbidden, tears drenched her eyes and she swiftly turned her head, cursing herself for her momentary weakness. "It's still a blank." Though considering the dreams she'd been having, she wondered if that would be true for much longer. Were they a prelude...a small break in the curtain concealing her past? It was a reasonable assumption.

He didn't comment, simply nodded. "In that case, have a seat, and I'll give you the grand tour."

"Again?" she said, managing a wry smile.

"Again," he confirmed.

"I'd like that." She fumbled in her skirt pocket for a pair of sunglasses to hide behind, suspecting it was too little, too late. Sebastian had already seen far more than she cared to reveal.

Turning the wheel, he opened the throttle wide, the speedboat slicing through the waves as it moved away from the yacht. He pointed toward a low section of the island and a cluster of small houses and buildings. "Only a couple of hundred people make their homes on *Rochefort*. Most live in the town that surrounds the harbor, though the reefs make approaching it tricky. But the islanders don't seem to mind. They say it discourages visitors."

She stared at him in concern. "Is that important?"

His expression turned enigmatic. "I suppose it depends on the visitor."

What did that mean? she couldn't help but wonder. "What do the villagers do for a living? Fish?"

"Some. Most farm. It's volcanic soil. You could stick a fence post in it and it would grow."

She grinned. "That's what they grow? Fence posts?"

"Very amusing, my sweet. The main crop is citrus, bananas and spices. But everyone has a vegetable garden. We like to stay as self-supporting as possible."

"And water? Isn't that a problem?"

He shook his head. "We're a lot like Dominica. We can even export water in times of crisis, though we're not set up for it."

The boat began to skirt the harbor and she glanced at him in confusion. "Don't we land at the village?" Treacherous or not, it appeared to be the only feasible harbor.

He shook his head, the wind tossing back his thick black hair, intensifying his roguish appearance. "You'll see."

They circled the island and she was struck anew with the untamed beauty of it. Coconut palms clung to the shoreline, marching up the steep folds of the mountains like an invading army, losing their ongoing battle with the denser vegetation. Huge smooth-skinned gommier trees marked swampier ground, birds flitting in and out of the canopy like butterflies in a garden.

When they were on the opposite side from the village, Sebastian headed in toward a sheer rocky cliff. "Hang on!" he shouted above the crash of the waves.

Anna didn't need a second warning, clinging to the armrests with white-knuckled fingers. She wanted desperately to close her eyes, but didn't. Her breath caught in her throat, and she waited for the screech of twisting metal, for the boat to be torn apart at the seams, certain they were going to crash against the deadly rocks ahead. At the last possible instant, he throttled back, allowing the waves to carry them between two jagged pillars. Then he ripped the engine wide open, jetting them over the crest of the swell and through an almost invisible break in the face of the mountainside.

She sat, stunned.

Before her lay the most beautiful scalloped lagoon she'd ever seen. The water was clear and a shade of blue that defied description. The beach surprised her. Instead of the dazzling white she'd grown accustomed to seeing, the sand here varied from a soft dove gray, to a deeper, smokier color wherever the waves danced across it. Palms shaded the beach and huge coconuts, still in their yellow-green husks, dotted the shore like fibrous boulders.

"Care to dive in?" Sebastian asked.

"Don't tempt me," she said with a laugh. She reached over the side, trailing a hand through the warm water. She could see clear down to the coral garden covering the ocean floor, fish of every size and description darting in and out of the reefs. "It's...it's unbelievable. How did you find it?"

He shot her a humorous glance. "I didn't. My ancestors settled the island. They landed not far from where the village is now. In time, they worked their way over the mountain to this side of the island and discovered the entrance to the lagoon. They found that a back door off the island came in handy."

She was tempted to ask what he meant, but something in his expression gave her pause. Instead she nodded. From somewhere a quote slipped into her head, and she repeated it, thinking it particularly apt.

"'When God made this place, He knew His job was done,'" she murmured.

He turned in a flash. "You've got the words right, though you've neglected to use the island dialect." His expression alarmed her, it was so sharp and cold.

She stiffened. "I . . . I don't understand."

"I thought you said your memory hadn't returned," he stated grimly. "Or is that why you're looking so delicate? Have you remembered?" He waited, resembling nothing more than a sleek, dangerous jungle cat poised to take down its prey. "Well . . . Have you?"

CHAPTER FIVE

ANNA stared at him in confusion. "I...I don't understand."

"That expression you used," Sebastian said. "It isn't yours."

"No, it isn't," she agreed, tilting her head to one side and attempting to recall where she'd heard it before. "It just came to me."

"It's an island expression. One they use here on *Rochefort*."

She stared at him, bewildered by his intensity. "If you say so," she said, adding with gentle emphasis, "I don't remember, Sebastian."

A strained moment ticked by, and slowly he relaxed. "But it would seem you're starting to remember. At least certain things."

She shrugged, pricked by a strange unease. "I guess. That's good, right?" She watched for the least change in his demeanor, hoping to determine whether he considered the return of her memory a positive event...or a negative one.

"Yes, Anna. Of course it's good," he reassured.

She bit down on her lip. "Are you sure?" she couldn't help but ask.

His eyes narrowed and he swiveled in his seat to look at her. "What do you mean?"

"I mean ... You accused me of faking my amnesia. You as good as told me there's some mystery surrounding the night of my accident, that I'd have to explain what actually transpired when I regained my memory. Which suggests..."

He watched her intently. "Suggests what?"

She sighed, reluctant to continue. Sebastian had described her as painfully direct, had made the assessment as though he considered it a positive character trait. Would he after this conversation? "It suggests that our marriage was in trouble."

He didn't say anything for a long moment. "If it was, you never confided as much to me," he finally said. "Now you tell me something. Do you think you're capable of marrying a man you didn't love?"

She stared in disbelief. "Are you serious?"

"Dead serious."

It didn't take any thought at all. Instinct took over, and she spoke with a heartfelt certainty. "I'd never give myself to a man unless I loved him with all my heart. And I wouldn't marry him unless he returned that love," she claimed.

"Then stop worrying," he said pointedly. "Stop looking for trouble. And promise you'll let me know if you remember anything else. I want your word on that, Anna."

Did that include the dreams? she wondered apprehensively. She'd really rather not have to mention those. "I'll do my best," she temporized. "It isn't always a major revelation. Things...things just occur to me in passing, like the quote."

"When they do, let me know."

He eased the boat toward a short wooden pier, docking with the speed of long practice. After securing the lines, they crossed to a shed that housed a rather battered Jeep.

"It's a long climb to the house," he explained in response to her surprised reaction. "When I was young, my grandfather used donkeys. Riding up the mountainside on their backs lost its appeal when I was in my twenties. So I retired the animals and brought in a fleet of Jeeps."

The Jeep had no doors or roof, only a hinged windscreen attached to the hood. She settled into the bucket seat and fastened her seat belt, eyeing the rough dirt road ahead with a frown. It wasn't much of a road, more a path, and it seemed to vanish into the dense undergrowth within feet of the forest's edge. "What about driving during inclement weather? Isn't it too hazardous?" she asked in concern.

He rested his forearms on the steering wheel. "Much too hazardous," he agreed. "The rivers overflow their banks and the road turns slick with mud. It's worth your neck to attempt this mountain." He paused to give weight to his demand. "You'll avoid doing anything so foolhardy."

She gripped her hands together, meeting his intense gray eyes with a haunted expression. "I've learned my lesson the hard way, Sebastian," she assured him in a low voice, the admission a painful one. "It's not one I'm likely to forget."

He didn't relent. "See that you don't." His voice dropped, each word stark with emotion. "You'll never know what it was like, seeing them rip open the mangled remains of that car in order to pry you out. You didn't move, didn't make a sound. I thought—" He broke off, staring across the lagoon, his jaw set in rigid lines.

"Oh, Sebastian," she whispered. "I had no idea."

His laugh was harsh and empty of humor. "Do you know the worst part?"

She caught her lower lip between her teeth and shook her head. "I can't imagine."

But she could. If their roles had been reversed, if she'd come upon such a horrendous accident, had witnessed the remains of the crash, been forced to stand by as the emergency personnel worked and seen Sebastian unconscious, critically injured... Her helplessness would have been the worst part, her inability to save him as she watched, powerless, as his life force drained slowly away. She shuddered, thrusting the horrifying images from her mind, refusing to dwell on it further.

His mouth tightened, his eyes almost black from the bleakness of his memories. "The worst part was, they wouldn't let me near you. Wouldn't let me touch you, see how severe the injuries were. I thought I'd go insane waiting to learn if you'd live or die."

Shaken, she couldn't say anything for a long moment, overwhelmed by his admission, by how closely aligned their fears were. "It's over," she tried to reassure. "Everything's all right now."

He shook his head. "It's not over, Anna. Not by a long shot."

"Because I can't remember?" she dared to ask.

He didn't reply. Instead, he started the engine, shooting her a sharp glance. "Just promise me you'll stay off the mountainside when the weather turns rough."

That would be an easy promise to keep. The mere thought of skidding down that treacherous road during a raging storm left her trembling in dread. "You have my word," she said.

With a nod of satisfaction, he set the Jeep in motion, plowing along the rough track. They wound in and out of dense jungle vegetation, laboring up the sides of pitching slopes before dodging back beneath towering mango and vine-covered turpentine trees.

Crossing a narrow wooden bridge, the musical chattering of a cascading river mingled with the cacophonous arguing of a flock of parakeets and the sweet trilling of a mountain whistler. Banana plants tumbled down the hillside to the river, joining flaming orange heliconia as well as the ferns and lianas scattered haphazardly on either side of the riverbank.

It took twenty minutes to gain the top of the mountain. Once there, Anna stared in wonder at the fortress built quite literally into the rock. "Dear heaven, Sebastian. Is this where you live?"

A teasing smile swept across his mouth. "No, my love. This is where *we* live."

She let the correction pass, awed by the sprawling grandeur of the estate. Curved stone walls were draped with deep rose-colored bougainvillea, and off to one side behind a crawler-entwined fence, she could see a neatly tended vegetable garden overflowing with beans, corn and melons. It was a veritable feast, ripe for the picking. Ahead of them lay the front entrance—a massive arching portal with double iron rings instead of doorknobs.

"It's huge!" she exclaimed. "When was it built?"

"In the early 1700s."

"That long ago?" She shook her head in amazement. "How could they possibly have managed?"

His expression turned grim. "The way many things were managed at that time. At great human expense and with a lot of blood and sweat."

It was a sad, unfortunate truth. "Even so, all this couldn't have been built back then," she said, gesturing toward the impressive stone structure.

"No, you're right. The central building is from that time period. Each successive generation has contributed to the rest until it's more octopus than house. Let's go in. I'm sure Dominique is awaiting our arrival."

He ushered her to the front entrance, pulling open the well-hinged door as though it weighed nothing at all. But she knew better. The solid wooden doors were ten feet tall and at least six inches thick. Whoever maintained their smooth operation had his work cut out for him.

Inside, the masonry walls provided a natural insulation, the entranceway cool and dim. The flooring was stone, worn smooth from centuries of foot traffic. Arched doorways led off in all directions. She glanced around in amazement, before focusing on a life-size portrait that dominated one wall.

She gasped, taking a swift, instinctive step backward, and bumping into Sebastian. He steadied her, gripping her shoulders with heavy hands and cradling her against the protective warmth of his body.

"What is it? What's wrong?"

"The portrait," she whispered, shocked. It was Sebastian. A Sebastian from centuries gone by. *A Sebastian she had seen in a drug-induced hallucination.* "It's you!"

He chuckled. "Not quite. It's my ancestor, Nicholas Kane."

She stared at the portrait in disbelief. "The resemblance is uncanny."

Even more remarkable was that every last detail was identical to the image she'd summoned in the hospital. Nicholas stood on the deck of a ship, *Rochefort* looming in the background. His hair fell to his shoulders in heavy curls, a red scarf banding his head. All he was missing was the proverbial black eye patch. But it was the half-raised cutlass that captured her attention. That, and his savage expression—an expression that was reckless and daring, full of ruthless intent.

She swallowed. "He's . . . He's a . . ."

"A pirate." Sebastian sounded amused. "Yes, I know."

So many minor details finally made sense. The hallucination at the hospital, Sebastian's comment about being a pirate, the need for a "back door" off the island. *Rochefort* had been settled by privateers led, no doubt, by Nicholas Kane. She found the knowledge unsettling.

But there was another fact that she found far more unsettling . . .

There could be no more lingering doubts about her marriage. She'd been here before. The portrait, alone, made that fact indisputable. No matter how unsettling she found it, Sebastian was unquestionably her husband. "That's what you meant when you said you were a pirate," she whispered.

"His blood runs in my veins." He turned her around to face him, his scar pulling his mouth to one side in a crooked smile. "Pirate's blood will run in our children's veins, too."

She stared at him, transfixed. "Children?"

His hand settled low on her stomach, his fingers stroking the taut, firm lines. "For all I know, you could be carrying my child right now."

She shook her head, shoving his hand away. "No! It's not possible."

He lifted a dark eyebrow. "No? Are you certain?"

Was she? she wondered in alarm. She had no idea when they'd last made love, what her cycle might be. Before she could consider the stunning possibility, a woman appeared beneath an archway, giving them a broad smile of greeting.

She was strikingly beautiful, tall and elegant, and boasting a mixed ancestry. Carib, African and European influences had all contributed to give her complexion a rich, *café au lait* color and lend an intriguing slant to her brown, almond-shaped eyes.

"I thought I heard that old rattletrap of a Jeep," she said, her words accented with a rolling calypso lilt. "Welcome home, Miss Anna! It is good to have you back where you belong."

"Anna, this is Dominique," Sebastian introduced them. "Our housekeeper."

Anna stepped forward and offered her hand. "You'll have to excuse me for not remembering. I'm afraid my memory is a little muddled from the accident."

She was subjected to a swift, piercing scrutiny. Then the housekeeper nodded. "Mr. Sebastian, he told me. Don't you worry none, mom. A few days of rest and some of Dominique's cooking and you'll be right as rain. You see if'n I'm not right."

"You always are," Sebastian said with a broad smile. "Has the luggage arrived?"

"Not yet. Josie called from the boat. They be along sooner rather than later. They want to make harbor before the storm." She clucked her tongue. "There be a wild one brewin' this night."

Anna couldn't prevent a shiver of apprehension. "Will it be bad?"

Dominique smiled reassuringly. "Don't you worry none, mom," she said again. "We batten down, no troubles. The winds won't find *Rocher Interdit*. Jes hol' strain."

"That means, relax," Sebastian murmured, slipping a comforting arm about Anna's waist. "We're going on a brief tour of the estate," he informed the housekeeper. "Can you manage an early dinner?"

Dominique inclined her head. "Something special, I think, to welcome Miss Anna home." With a flashing smile, she disappeared into the far recesses of the house, her sandals a soft whisper on the uneven flagstones.

Sebastian looked down at Anna. "Are you up to a tour? We won't walk far, just through the gardens and to the Needle."

"The Needle?"

"It's a lookout."

"Over the ocean?" she asked, her interest piqued.

"It's a necessary precaution when one's a pirate," he replied, a humorous gleam turning his eyes to silver.

She nodded, eager for a glimpse of the promised view. "I'd like that."

A lazy smile spread across his face and she caught her breath at the change it made. She'd never seen him more relaxed, more in his element. The tension had disappeared. And though she'd never accuse him of being soft, he wasn't as hard or remote, nor as

guarded as he'd been. But then, why would he be?
He had everything he wanted. She'd come to his pirate's retreat, and from what little she'd seen so far,
getting off again wouldn't be a simple task. She
glanced at him, hoping she successfully hid her
thoughts. For one final question remained, domi-
nating all other concerns.

What more did he expect from her?

She slipped free of his hold, knowing she wouldn't
so easily slip free of whatever else he had planned.
"Shall we go?" she asked.

"It's this way."

He led her into the cool interior of the house,
through vaulted entranceways and along sun-dappled
corridors. It was a veritable maze and she had no idea
how she'd ever find her way again. Had she learned
it before? At last they came to an outer door that
opened onto the garden she'd seen earlier. Close to
the house, beneath the shade of a nutmeg tree was a
herb garden, further out, a veritable cornucopia of
fruits and vegetables.

He indicated the profusion of plants. "This is
Dominique's province. Disturb it at your own risk."

"I don't even recognize half of what's out here,"
she marveled.

"Well, you'll get to taste most of it. Dominique's
culinary skills are renowned throughout the islands."

They wandered past the well-ordered garden to a
wrought-iron gate on the far side. A rocky path
climbed toward a promontory that jutted out from
the surrounding forest to hang above the surging
ocean. She didn't see the tower at first, it was so well
disguised by the surrounding vegetation. It rose be-

tween twin trees like a slender reed, dark and vine-entangled.

"Is it safe?" she asked.

"I had the structure strengthened after the last hurricane. Do you want to climb it?"

It was tempting, despite the heat. "How's the view?"

"Spectacular. Well worth the climb."

He pushed open the door at the base and ushered her inside. The dim interior was a stark contrast to the brilliant sunshine and she blinked, hesitating just inside the doorway while her vision adjusted. An anole clung to the wall, pinpricks of white speckling its slender, bark-brown body. It stared at them for a moment, distending its yellowish-orange throat in warning. Then it skittered off through a window slit.

Sebastian glanced down at her, a teasing smile touching his mouth. "Still willing to climb to the top?"

She nodded, returning his grin. "Lizards don't bother me. Snakes might present a problem, if any are lurking in corners."

"As I remember, it was a Hercules beetle that sent you flying into my arms during our last visit."

She stilled. "We were here before?"

He closed the distance between them, his broad shoulders eclipsing the light streaming in from the doorway. "We climbed the Needle our second day here."

"I wish I could remember," she whispered, gazing up the spiraling steps that disappeared into the beckoning darkness.

"You will."

"And when I do?" She glanced over her shoulder at him, struggling to analyze his expression. But his thoughts remained cloaked.

"When you do, we'll have a few things to talk about."

"That sounds ominous," she managed to say.

He shrugged, refusing to comment further. "Do you want to go first, or shall I?"

"I will."

She climbed, her eyes having adjusted to the gloom, following in the footsteps of countless before her. Thin shafts of light spilled from the narrow windows, bouncing off the whitewashed walls and capturing the dust motes spinning in the still air. Sebastian followed right behind, silent and protective, his hand close to hers on the rail. Between his overpowering presence and the seemingly endless flight of stairs, she was breathless by the time she reached the narrow ladder that led out onto the top walkway.

She pulled herself through the trap door, dusting her skirt and lifting her hair off her damp neck. But as soon as she straightened and looked around, she forgot her discomfort. She'd never seen anything as beautiful as this. She crossed to the railing, overwhelmed, not knowing where to look first.

"Oh, Sebastian," she murmured, letting her breath out in a long sigh.

"I told you it would be worth the climb."

Below, she could see the twisting road they'd taken to reach the house, the switchbacks winding in and out of the rain forest like a discarded ribbon. Directly beneath them, the sun-washed beach looked inviting. Odd, sparkling patterns appeared in the dark, volcanic sand before disappearing and reforming with each ensuing wave. It mesmerized her and she could have watched the constantly changing images for hours.

The ocean was intensely blue, hissing against the shore, a stark contrast to the waves foaming about the narrow ingress they'd traversed to reach the lagoon. There, it battered the jagged rocks. And further out was the endless ocean, crystal clear and empty of ships all the way to the horizon.

"It's spectacular. Thank you for bringing me," she said, twisting around to look up at him. "I can see why Nicholas built the tower. It's the perfect defense. Anyone approaching this side of the island would be instantly spotted. But what if they attacked from the other side?"

"When Nicholas first settled here, he constructed a series of towers around the island," Sebastian explained. He gestured to a chain hooked to the pillar at her left. "They were manned at all times. If trouble was sighted, a warning bell would be sounded to alert the household and the village."

"Surely they couldn't hear the bell all the way to the village."

Sebastian shook his head. "It didn't have to be heard that far, only to the next watchtower. The warning would be carried around the island by bell. Nicholas also developed a code—a specific series of rings—to inform his pirate confederates which watchtower had spotted the danger, the source of the trouble, and even what response he required."

"It sounds like an effective system," she commented, impressed.

"It was. Men wrote of the bells—the Bells of Doom, they were called. It was an effective deterrent to invasion. *Rochefort* never once fell to outsiders."

Which reminded her... "What did Dominique call the island? It wasn't *Rochefort*."

"*Rocher Interdit*. It was the original name of the island when Nicholas first settled here. The islanders still call it that instead of *Rochefort*."

"What does it mean?"

"Forbidden Rock."

She shivered. Actually, it seemed a more appropriate name than the present one. "Why did he change it?"

"He didn't. His descendants did. When they decided to go legit, they thought it would help their cause to have a less sinister name for the island."

"What cause?"

"The larger islands were being fought over by the French and British. And though we're off the beaten path, the family feared their claim to *Rochefort* wouldn't be recognized. So they curried favor with the British empire by helping them defeat the French. As a sign of appreciation the British government made the family's claim official."

"The Kanes sided with the British?" she questioned, confused. "But the island's name is French."

He shrugged. "The blood of many nations runs through our veins. Nicholas's mother was French, while his wife was a Duchess, a prize he stole from one of the British ships he attacked. Even when a fortune in ransom was offered, he refused to release her."

"Or perhaps she refused to go," Anna guessed. Sneaking a glance at Sebastian, she could guess why the Duchess had stayed. For all their hardness, the Kane men held an undeniable attraction that could neither be ignored nor denied.

"You could be right. Their journals indicate they shared an unparalleled love. Nicholas's son also chose well. He took a Spanish wife, his grandson preferred a Portuguese beauty."

"And you?" she dared to ask.

His smile faded, his gaze growing dark and heated. "I chose a mysterious amber jewel for my wife, a woman of warmth and passion with a fierce inner fire."

She stared up at him, a strange yearning taking hold. "Are you trying to seduce me again?" she whispered.

"Is it working?"

"Yes," she confessed. "I envy you all this, you know. The sense of history and belonging. Knowing who your family was. I have nothing. No memories, no connections."

"You have me. And I can tell you what I know of your background." He slid his arms around her, tucking her close. "You grew up in Florida, near Tallahassee. Your father died when you were young. And your mother was a nurse. When you were little, you longed for brothers and sisters and you used to bribe your girlfriends to be your sister for a day. You collected stray cats and your favorite was a ragged-ear tiger named Creeper. You have a weakness for red lollipops. You adore black and white movies. And you give the sweetest kisses of anyone I know."

Tears pricked her eyes and she gave him a tremulous smile. "Thank you for telling me that," she whispered. "It means a lot."

"It will all come back to you, Anna. I promise." He gazed down at her, a frown touching his brow. "You're looking tired," he commented. "Would you like to shower and rest? Or does a swim appeal?"

As tempted as she was by the offer of a swim and a visit to the lagoon, the thought of an hour's nap appealed even more. Too many sleepless nights had left her exhausted. Perhaps being on *Rochefort* and having Sebastian close at hand would ease the terrifying nightmares that haunted her. She gripped her hands together, unwilling to analyze why she thought that. All she knew for certain was that something would have to give soon, because she didn't know how much more she could take.

"Could we save a visit to the lagoon for tomorrow?" she suggested.

He inclined his head. "Of course. Your luggage should have arrived by now. I'll go down first. It can be awkward your first couple of times."

"Thanks. I'd appreciate that."

He disappeared through the open trap door and then called to her. "Okay. The way's clear."

She took a final look around. The land was so beautiful, so fierce and untamed. So much like Sebastian. She nibbled on her lower lip. And so very different from anything she considered safe or familiar. Crossing to the hatchway, she knelt beside the dark opening.

"I'm here," she said.

"Hold on to the edges and slide your foot down. The step's right under you."

Following his quiet directions, she found the first rung, relieved to feel his hands at her waist guiding her down the steep, narrow ladder. At last she stepped off the final rung and straight into his arms.

Outside she could hear the shrill screeching of the birds and the insistent clicks and whirs of countless insects. The wind stirred the palm fronds, the restless rasp of leaf against leaf exciting an inexplicable agitation. A part of her was acutely aware of those sounds, their strangeness, their intensity, the peculiar effect they had on her. But the other part of her was tightly focused on the man who held her.

She stared at him, the outer wildness adding to her inner tension, her emotions growing more and more strained. The atmosphere stilled, a sultry warmth swirling about them. She could hear every breath he drew, the harsh sound magnified by the rounded walls.

"Anna," he murmured, his whisper reverberating through the tower like a silvery sigh.

Then he kissed her, while the jungle called to them, throbbing in their blood, pulsating with a primitive beat that echoed the thunder of their hearts. He molded her against him, his leg thrust between her thighs in a blatantly sexual embrace, firing a passion that had been smoldering just beneath the surface.

He offered no reprieve, but demanded a response, a response that came as naturally to her as the waves crashing to the shore far below. She surrendered to him, unable to resist the hot lure of his mouth or his slow, heated caresses. And in that brief moment, she knew...

She knew she wasn't alone and unconnected anymore. She knew she'd finally come home.

CHAPTER SIX

ANNA didn't remember leaving the watchtower or returning to "the fortress"—as she'd privately dubbed the huge house and estate. All her thoughts were focused on Sebastian and that kiss. That amazing, mind-blowing kiss.

How was it possible that he had such a stunning effect on her, that he could sweep away every thought, every ounce of resistance with a single touch? She didn't understand it. Unless... She shook her head, shying from a sudden, startling thought. Could she...*love* Sebastian, the feelings asserting themselves despite her memory loss?

No. It was crazy. Love had no part in this equation. How could she love someone when she had no memory to reinforce that love? And how could such intense emotions persist and she not remember the man involved? It didn't seem feasible. And yet... What other possible explanation could there be for her reaction? Because every time he came near, her opposition melted away like frost beneath a scorching sun.

She walked into the bedroom he indicated and stopped dead, waking to her surroundings with shocking immediacy.

"Oh, no. Not a chance," she exclaimed, taking a hasty step backward. "I'm not sleeping here."

"What's wrong?"

She spun around and glared at him. "You know what's wrong." She gestured to encompass everything from the personal articles scattered on the dresser to the king-size bed. "This is your room."

"Our room," he corrected, planting himself in front of the doorway and effectively blocking her retreat.

She shook her head, her mouth a straight, tense line. "I don't think so."

"I do." His stance remained rock-solid, a silent warning that they weren't going anywhere until they'd settled this latest argument. He folded his arms across his chest. "We've shared this room before. We'll share it now. You're getting upset about nothing."

She pointed at the bed. "*That* is not nothing!"

A slow grin etched a path across his mouth. "We're in complete agreement there. Making love should never be easy to dismiss."

She studied him warily, fighting the instinct that urged her to push past him and flee. Only one thing kept her rooted to the spot—the knowledge that should she attempt to leave he'd stop her, physically restrain her, if necessary. And she didn't want that to happen. Not here. Not now. Not while that jungle-cat gleam lurked in his eyes and the bed could be reached in three swift steps.

"I could take you," he murmured, accurately interpreting the reason for her anxiety. "I could sweep you into my arms and carry you to that bed."

She stiffened. "I wouldn't advise it. Not unless you want me screaming the house down," she bluffed. "And not unless you plan on using force. Because that's the only way you'll succeed."

He laughed, a dark, husky sound that rumbled deep in his chest and held her with mesmerizing power. "Force? Oh, no, my love. Never that."

She lifted her chin. "What would you call it? You're trying to coerce me into doing something I'd rather not do. That requires the use of force."

"Your lack of experience is appalling," he informed her, clearly amused. "I'll have to see if I can't change that."

Lack of experience? She raised a questioning eyebrow. How much experience did it take to know that the only way he'd get her in his bed was by literally picking her up and putting her there—unless he knew something she didn't? She stared at him uncertainly. Never had she felt so vulnerable, so out of her element. In one easy move he'd cut through her defenses to expose a weakness she hadn't realized existed.

"I have no idea what you're talking about," she said, struggling to recover her equilibrium.

An odd expression darkened his face, deepening the gray of his eyes. "I'm well aware of that, my love. But you will. I'll make sure of it. You want to know how a man gets a woman in bed without using physical coercion? Well, listen, and I'll tell you."

She didn't like the sound of this. "Sebastian—"

"You're not listening," he cut her off. "Now pay attention. Lesson one. Only very violent and insecure men need to resort to something as crass as force. And I am neither violent nor insecure. Merely driven."

"I don't want to hear this—"

"Lesson two," he continued as though she hadn't interrupted. "Persuasion is a useful tool when confronted with obstinacy."

Obstinacy? She'd show him obstinate. "Persuasion only works on those who can be persuaded," she stated with surprising composure. "I'm not one who can be."

"Are you sure?" He crooked a finger. "Why don't you come here and we'll make certain?"

She took a hasty step backward, her poise threatening to desert her. "I'm not that foolish," she informed him.

He shrugged, dropping his hands to his sides, something in his posture and in the intentness of his gaze filling her with a vague sense of alarm. "Lesson three. If persuasion fails, try temptation."

"I'm not in the least tempted," she lied, not quite certain why she'd started to ease away from him. But some gut instinct warned that she should put space between the two of them.

"How do you know? You haven't heard my offer. Come closer and I'll whisper it in your ear."

She shot a nervous glance toward the bed. "If it involves this room or any of the furniture in this room, I'll have to decline."

"I'm open to creative expression." He cocked an eyebrow. "Which room would you like to use? Any with a counter, couch, rug or chair is fine with me. Or is a natural setting more to your liking? Say, making love on the beach beneath a star-filled sky?"

Her cheeks flamed and she shook her head, incapable of uttering a single word.

"No? Then we'll move on to lesson four." He left the doorway and approached, following as she retreated, stalking with all the grace and skill of a panther. "When all else fails...try seduction."

She shot out of reach, stumbling in her efforts to evade him. "Sebastian, please. Don't do this."

He caught her before she fell, wrapping her in his arms as though she were the most precious of treasures. "Don't do what?" he mocked gently. "Hold you? Kiss you?" His voice deepened. "Seduce you?"

"No. Don't do any of that," she agreed, fighting the traitorous desires that signaled just the opposite. "I don't want it."

"Liar."

"I can't deal with it right now."

Laughter creased his face. "You don't have to. Just lay back and let me deal with everything."

"You can't realistically expect me to sleep with you," she tried again.

He tilted his head to one side, his gray eyes gleaming with fierce determination. "Can't I?"

"No! It's unreasonable." She fought his hold, feeling like a rabbit caught in the jaws of a wolf. He might be playful now, but that wouldn't save her in the long run.

"I think it's quite reasonable." His arms tightened, bringing her against the lean, taut length of him, branding her with both touch and gaze. "I'm your husband. You're my wife. One night in that bed and you won't find it unreasonable ever again."

She refused to back down, anger giving her the courage to defy him. "So you're demanding your conjugal rights, regardless of what I want?"

"If you choose to put it that way... Yes. Though it is what you want, no matter how much you deny it. You give yourself away every time I touch you. Shall I prove it to you?"

"No! Don't bother." She wouldn't attempt to debate his statement. How could she? He spoke the truth. "What if I refuse to cooperate?"

"You won't refuse for long." Desire tightened the skin across his high cheekbones and gave his words a rough, husky edge. "Why fight me on this? You want me. I want you. Our kiss in the watchtower proved that much. It's all quite simple."

"That kiss changes nothing," she declared. "And it's not the least bit simple."

"We're married, Anna," he reminded her impatiently. "How much more simple can it get? Or have you forgotten that minor detail?"

She offered a cool smile. "As a matter of fact, I have forgotten. And no amount of seduction is going to help me remember."

There was a long, tense silence. "I will seduce you, my sweet," he informed her.

She shook her head. "I don't think so."

An odd compassion swept across his features, belying the decisiveness of his tone. "I will because you want to be seduced. You're just afraid to admit it. Somewhere, buried deep in your subconscious, imprinted on your very soul is what we once shared. And one of these nights, with only the moon and stars looking on, I'll take you in my arms and join with you on that bed. And you will remember that you belong to me."

His words had a devastating effect, sweeping past the protective barriers she'd erected with frightening ease. "Please, Sebastian." Her hands clenched in the soft cotton of his shirt. "Don't do this."

"I must."

She didn't want to plead with him, didn't want him to realize how vulnerable she felt, how uncertain she was of her ability to resist him. "But, don't you see? Making love to you would be paramount to making love to a stranger."

He didn't relent. "I'm not a stranger."

"You are to me! Doesn't it matter that I have no memory of you? No memory that I married you... loved you."

Deep grooves carved a path alongside his mouth, his scar a streak of white across his cheek. "It matters. You'll never know how much."

She stared at him with a wrenching wistfulness. "And did I? Did I love you?"

A muscle jerked in his jaw. "I thought so."

"But you're not sure, are you?"

He didn't answer right away. Finally, he spoke, his gaze turned inward, a weary resignation shading his words. "Our last night on the island we made love in that bed. You lay beneath me, bathed in a pool of moonlight that gilded your hair and turned your skin to pure silver. And you looked up at me, your eyes like golden flames, and you told me you loved me more than life itself." He focused on her, his emotions tamped, his cool reserve once more in place. "Were you lying?"

"I don't know," she confessed, stricken.

"Don't you?" he questioned skeptically. He released his breath in a gusty sigh. "It doesn't matter whether or not you were. You're my wife, Anna." He stated the fact with unrelenting finality. "That's all that matters."

"But, I don't remember," she whispered. "I may never remember."

His grip tightened. "What if you don't? Are we supposed to treat each other like polite strangers for the rest of our lives? That's not going to work and you know it."

She caught her lower lip between her teeth. "I . . . I realize that. But . . . We can't just pick up where we left off. You're a man who likes to be in control and I won't be controlled. Not with words. And not with sex."

She could feel the anger that swept through him, his tension clear in the tight line of his jaw and fierce light in his eyes. "Then what do you propose?" he demanded.

"Perhaps we could start over," she suggested tentatively. "We could get to know each other the way we did before, fall in love all over again."

He gave a short laugh. "You don't ask much, do you?"

She gazed up at him, wondering if her hope was reflected in her eyes. "But we could do that, couldn't we? Start over? Perhaps it would even help me regain my memory."

"What do you mean?"

"We . . . we enjoyed our time here, didn't we?"

"You could say that," came his dry response.

"What if we recreated some of the incidents? Perhaps it would help spark a memory."

"We did more than climb the Needle and swim in the lagoon," he warned.

She didn't pretend to misunderstand. "We made love."

"Yes. We made love." Urgency deepened his voice. "Let me show you. You won't regret it."

Wouldn't she? A great, mysterious gulf separated them and until she'd discovered why, she didn't dare sleep with him. It would be too final and irrevocable a step. She shook her head, easing from his embrace. "Not yet. Not until I know you better."

He released her, his hands sliding along her hips in a final, intimate caress. "We could try it your way. For the time being, anyway," he agreed, a wry smile twisting his mouth. "I assume you'll want separate rooms."

She gripped her hands together. "Yes," she said with devastating candor, managing to look him straight in the eye.

"You realize I won't wait forever."

"I do realize that."

"There's one more thing." He held her with a single, razor-sharp gaze. "I still haven't decided whether or not your memory loss is real. So we'll continue to play this game your way... for now. But one of these days you're going to have to face the past. And when that day arrives, the time for games will be over."

She met his gaze unflinchingly. "I'm well aware of that."

"I hope so. Because recreating our courtship isn't going to change a thing—not once I'm certain you have your memory back."

"What happened to us, Sebastian?" she questioned urgently. "Tell me!"

He shook his head. "I've already told you. It's you who will have to explain what happened. And now I'll show you to your room." With that, he turned on his heel and strode from the room.

Anna had no choice but to follow. But once again she was confronted with the disturbing knowledge that he didn't believe her...and that whatever had set them at odds was serious.

Very serious.

"Anna. Anna, wake up."

"No... Not..."

"Anna."

"What...?" She opened her eyes, thoroughly disoriented, the unfamiliar surroundings confusing her. Shadows draped the room in shifting shades of gray and she fastened on the only familiar object she could see. "Bastian?" she whispered, oddly comforted by his presence.

He crossed to sit beside her on the bed. "Yes, sweetheart. It's me."

"I fell asleep," she said, stating the obvious. "What time is it?"

"It's late. Dominique held dinner, but I didn't think it wise to let you sleep any longer. Not if you expect to get any rest tonight."

"It doesn't matter," she admitted thoughtlessly. She tossed aside the sheet and sat up, curling her legs beneath her. "I always have trouble sleeping at night."

He brushed her bangs from her face, his touch lingering on the small, puckered scar at her temple. "And why is that?"

She shrugged, her gaze slipping from his. She'd unwittingly revealed far too much—which wasn't the wisest course of action with Sebastian. "I just do. What's for dinner?" she asked, hoping to change the subject.

To her relief, he allowed the diversion. "Knowing Dominique, it'll be one of your favorites. She likes to pamper."

Anna nodded. "Give me five minutes to freshen up and I'll be down."

He shook his head. "I'll wait for you. I don't want you to get lost."

Knowing it would prove fruitless to argue, she didn't waste any time, but hastened to repair her hair and makeup. Next she changed into an informal strapless dress in a dramatic red, the pleated skirt floating lightly about her knees. "I'm ready," she announced, slipping on a pair of heels.

He stared at her, his appreciative gaze distinctly male. "You look stunning," he told her in a husky voice.

Suddenly the room felt close and warm, the air heavy, making each breath she drew a monumental task. She hesitated, sensing the dangerous undercurrents that charged the atmosphere. A choice loomed before her. She could stay here and incur all the risks that would entail. Or she could flee.

The temptation to linger nearly overwhelmed her. And Sebastian, damn him, knew it, a slow, perceptive smile edging his mouth. Without a word, she turned and left the room, refusing to allow insanity to prevail. Sebastian followed at a more leisurely pace and she didn't dare look to see his reaction to her decision. But aside from a brief, knowing chuckle, he didn't comment.

They headed down the steps together. To her surprise, he bypassed the formal dining room, and led the way to a screened terrace overlooking the garden. Flowers skirted the area in dense profusion and a table set for two held center stage. Dominique clearly had romance in mind when she'd planned their dinner. Deep red candles illuminated the table, the soft pool of light imbuing the crystal and silver with a warm, translucent glow. As a centerpiece, delicate white orchids and crimson hibiscus blossoms floated in a pool of scented water.

Sebastian held out a chair. "Have a seat."

"It's lovely," Anna murmured. She ran her hand over the heavy linen tablecloth. Age had mellowed the color to a deep ivory and she caught the faint scent of the lavender in which it had been stored.

He lifted an eyebrow. "You did say you'd like to recreate our time together, didn't you?"

She stilled as the full significance of his comment sank in. "We've dined like this before?" she questioned, gesturing to encompass the table and flowers. "You and Dominique set this up deliberately?"

He tilted his head to one side in a gesture that was fast becoming endearingly familiar. "Isn't that what you wanted?"

She fought the tightness closing her throat. "You know it is. But you said you didn't believe me. So why...?"

"I said I wasn't totally convinced you'd lost your memory," he corrected, opening the bottle of *Sancerre* at his elbow and pouring her a glass. He uncovered a platter containing a selection of turnovers. "They're *empanadas*," he said. "Pastries stuffed with chicken and seafood."

"They look delicious," she admitted. "But you still haven't told me why you're doing this."

He hesitated, his dark gray eyes filled with a strange reserve. "Because you asked."

She could hardly take it in. "You did all this . . . for me?"

"I did all this . . . for us."

Unexpected tears pricked her eyes. "Sebastian—"

"It was a simple enough request to grant," he said with a shrug. "And it was my pleasure to do it for you."

She lowered her eyes, deeply moved. "Thank you," she whispered. "This means a lot to me."

He broke off a flaky piece of the steaming pastry and offered it to her. "Relax and enjoy the evening, my love," he urged gently. "Let nature take its course. A few days of leisure will do us both some good."

Sebastian was right, she realized. It was past time she allowed nature to take its course. Since he planned to indulge her request, she'd follow his lead. And maybe something would occur to prod her memory.

She nibbled on the spicy appetizer and took a sip of wine, delighting in the light, dry flavor. A gentle breeze stirred the air, brushing across her bare shoulders with a velvety warmth. The flames of the candles flickered, the light chasing the darkness in a brief, capricious dance. For an instant the silvery scar curling across Sebastian's cheek stood out in stark relief, then it vanished into shadow, leaving behind the perfection of tautly sculpted features.

She didn't mind his scar, in fact she found it rather appealing. She touched her temple self-consciously. The same couldn't be said of hers. Did it bother him? Did he find her less attractive because of it?

He noticed her action and a small frown pulled at his brows. "It'll fade in time. You should be proud of it. It marks you as a survivor."

"It doesn't bother me," she claimed, dropping her hand, then sighed. "Well . . . Not much." She glanced at his cheek. "How were you injured?"

"In a plane accident."

She gasped and her arm jerked reflexively, knocking over her wineglass. Sebastian caught the fragile crystal before it hit the floor. Mopping up the wine, he repositioned the glass toward the center of the table.

He lifted a questioning eyebrow. "Are you okay?"

She stared at him mutely, unable to explain the severity of her reaction to herself, let alone to him. Finally she found her voice. "I'm sorry," she whispered, choking on the words. "You caught me off guard. What happened? How did you crash?"

He shrugged, refilling her glass. "I was sixteen and trying out a new plane. The engine quit."

The muscles in her stomach clenched, and her heart raced as though she'd run a mile. She held out her hands. "Look at me," she said with a breathless laugh. "I'm shaking. Silly, isn't it?"

His gaze grew tender. "It's all right, Anna. Let it go. It happened a long time ago. I'm here, safe and sound, with only this—" He fingered his cheek. "—to remind me of my foolishness. And it worked out for the best in the long run. The accident determined my future."

"How is that?" She reached for the wine, picking up the glass with great care and taking a quick, restorative sip.

"The malfunction turned out to be a design flaw. I found the investigation and repairs so intriguing, I decided that was what I wanted to do—design and build planes. Only mine would be flawless, tested with scrupulous care."

"And it's worked out?"

He inclined his head. "Until a recent problem cropped up."

"Is this recent problem what kept you from returning to *Rochefort* with me?" she asked.

"Yes. Over a year ago there was a fatal accident involving my last design," he explained reluctantly. "It's prompted a lawsuit."

"But you weren't at fault." It wasn't a question. A gut instinct told her he wasn't to blame.

His expression warmed. "You're so certain?"

She thought about it, realizing with a dawning sense of wonder that she had no doubts whatsoever. "Yes," she replied simply. "I'm positive."

He nodded. "You're right. Every aspect of the accident was investigated. After months of tests, the authorities cleared me of any responsibility. They attributed the crash to pilot error."

"But this man who's suing you..."

"Samuel."

"Samuel isn't satisfied?"

"It was his parents who were killed and he refuses to concede the possibility of pilot error."

Compassion touched her. "That's sad. He's obviously blinded by his grief. Is there no way you can satisfy him and prove your innocence?"

He shook his head. "He wants the engineering data and test pilot reports for the plane. But that information is valuable, and I'm not about to let it out of my possession. Not when I'd have no control over its disposition. There's a lot of unscrupulous people who would pay top dollar for it. And I refuse to allow them to profit off my hard work."

"Will it go to court?"

"It's been thrown out of court once already, a few months ago. I'd hoped that would end the matter. But he's making noises again, contacting the media in the hope of forcing the issue."

"What are you going to do?"

"I've arranged to bring in an independent investigator, one whose reputation is above reproach. With luck, that will settle the matter."

Dominique appeared in the doorway, pushing a cart. "What is this?" she demanded, frowning at them. "You talk business when romance is in the air? That don't do nobody no good."

Anna smiled. "You're right. No more business talk."

"That's for damn sure." Dominique removed the few remaining *empanadas* and replaced them with several platters from her cart. "*Crabe farci*," she announced. "You always say they be your favorite."

"It looks delicious," Anna informed her warmly. "Thank you."

Dominique beamed in delight. "You eat now. Enjoy." Whisking away the used plates, she left them to their own devises.

"Do you remember the dish?" Sebastian asked quietly.

Anna shook her head, unable to meet his eyes. "It's a unique experience," she said, attempting a smile. "I can enjoy it for the first time all over again."

If he heard the betraying catch in her voice, he didn't comment. "These are land crabs," he explained, serving her the crab as well as a selection of fruits. "They live beneath the coconut palms. Dominique collects them and then restricts their diet to pepper leaves for several days."

"Pepper leaves?" she questioned, grateful to him for the respite so she could bring her emotions back under control. "Why?"

"It acts as a purge and enriches the taste. Then they're picked, seasoned and baked in the shell. Try it."

She scooped out a sampling of meat. It practically melted on her tongue. "This is wonderful!"

"Now have some pineapple with it."

He held out a sliver and, after a momentary hesitation, she allowed him to feed it to her, too aware of the provocative undertones to even taste the sweetness of the fruit. She swallowed, unable to move, barely able to breathe. His thumb brushed her lower lip, catching a droplet of juice. And then, before she suspected what he was about, he leaned forward and captured her mouth in a swift, light kiss.

She pulled back, staring at him wide-eyed. "You promised," she began.

"Yes, I promised," he agreed. "I promised to re-enact our time here. And that's what I'm doing."

The words seemed straightforward enough, but she sensed a deeper meaning, a wealth of shading that extended far below the surface comment. "And this reenactment includes kissing me?" she demanded.

"Of course." A slow smile crept across his mouth and his eyes were alight with secrets. He speared a succulent morsel of passion fruit and offered it to her, laughing when she stubbornly refused. "You're right, you know. This is a unique experience. We can relive our past as though it were for the first time. The first time ... again."

"Meaning ... ?"

He leaned forward, the intensity of his regard capturing her full attention. "Did you think I kept my distance before? I didn't. I was ruthless in my pursuit of you. I seduced you then. And I'll do it again now. If not tonight, then tomorrow. Or the next night. Or the one after that. Are you prepared to resist temptation night after night?"

"Yes!"

He didn't look annoyed, as she half expected. If anything, he looked amused. "In that case, it would appear history is certain to repeat itself," he murmured, picking up his crab shell and forking out the last of the meat.

"Why do you say that?" she demanded.

A sudden gust of wind ripped across the terrace, the first manifestation of the storm Dominique had mentioned. The candles leapt wildly, shadows careening in frenzied abandon. "Because," he finally answered. "That's also what you said last time."

She should feel nervous, threatened. Instead she found herself wishing he'd kiss her one more time so that she could savor the sweetness of pineapple on his lips and feel his fingers caressing her mouth. Dismayed by her treacherous thoughts, she dropped her gaze to her plate, forcing herself to focus on her meal. But as delicious as the crab tasted, Sebastian's kiss had tasted even better.

I seduced you then. And I'll do it again now. She couldn't get his words out of her head, couldn't help wondering exactly what they'd done—what *he'd* done. It maddened her, that he knew so much about her... had known her in the fullest sense of the word and she remembered nothing about it. Worse, he wouldn't tell her the details, leaving her totally vulnerable. She pushed crabmeat around the inside of the shell, her appetite gone. Perhaps her suggestion—and his agreement—were more of a risk than she'd anticipated. She peeked at him through her lashes.

He met her gaze with calm equanimity. "Eat," he prompted. "You need your strength."

"You don't make it easy," she murmured.

"That wasn't my intention. Here." He cut a slice of a creamy cheese covered in grape seeds. "It's called *grappe*. Try this while we discuss our plans for tomorrow."

He kept the conversation light and relaxing from then on. By the end of the meal Anna found she'd finished the crab, several servings of the *grappe*, and part of a custard flavored with soursop, a fruit grown by the villagers. It was late by the time the last dish was removed. The candles had long since guttered, leaving them in semidarkness, the moonlight coming and going from behind scuttling clouds.

"You should turn in," Sebastian said at last. "We've a busy day tomorrow."

She finished the tea Dominique had served, one brewed with herbs from her garden and guaranteed to ensure a restful night. "A trip to the village and the airstrip, right? I'm looking forward to it."

He stood. "I'll walk you to your room."

"It's not necessary," she instantly protested, slipping from her chair.

"Yes. It is."

She didn't bother arguing. They retraced their steps and she was delighted to discover that she remembered the way. They paused outside her door and he took her into his arms, his hold gentle, his fingertips tracing the line from shoulder to collarbone.

"You remind me of honey," he observed softly. "The color of your hair, the silkiness of your skin, the clear purity of your eyes. It's like amber shot with sunlight."

"And you remind me of the island. Hard, dark, volcanic."

He chuckled. "You aren't the first to make the comparison."

She returned his smile. "I doubt I'll be the last, either." To her surprise, he released her. She stared at him in bewilderment, knowing she should be relieved that he'd made no attempt to kiss her. Instead she felt the acute tug of disappointment.

"There's a storm moving in," he reminded. He tilted her chin, caressing the rounded curve of her jaw. "Are you going to be all right?"

"Of course," she lied. "Storms don't bother me."

He inclined his head. "In that case, sleep well. You know where I am if you need me."

She took a quick step back and his hand fell away. "Thank you, but I won't need you." She opened the door and slipped across the threshold. "Good night, Sebastian."

He stood in the hallway, unmoving, and it was then that she realized just how serious a threat he posed. She'd wanted his kiss, had expected it, anticipated it. And now all she felt was a gnawing emptiness. Did he know? she wondered. Did he suspect how tempted she was to invite him in, to lose herself in the strength of his arms, the passion of his kisses, to surrender everything?

He smiled then, a smile of blatant seduction, his unwavering gaze a wicked enticement.

And she realized that he didn't just suspect how close she'd come to surrender . . . he knew.

The storm hit on the stroke of midnight, carrying the nightmares within its roaring winds.

CHAPTER SEVEN

ANNA'S door crashed open, rocking on its hinges.

"*Bastian!*" Her cry was one of terror and panic.

He was beside her in an instant, sweeping her into his arms, his touch a blissful slice of heaven in the midst of hellish despair. "I'm here, sweetheart. I'm here."

"I keep seeing it," she said, crying uncontrollably. Hysteria edged ever closer, and she didn't know how much longer she could hold it at bay. "The accident. It keeps replaying over and over. I can't get it out of my head. Please! Make it go away. Make it stop!"

His arms tightened. "Listen to me, Anna. The accident's in the past. It can't hurt you anymore. You're safe now. I'm with you and you're safe."

He reached out and turned on the bedside lamp. Light bathed them in a warm, reassuring glow. He held her for a long time, talking nonsense while she wept. Gradually she gained control, the tears coming to a slow end.

"I'm sorry," she whispered, wiping her cheeks. "I didn't mean to disturb you."

"It's the storm, isn't it?" he asked. "It's brought back memories of the accident."

She burrowed deeper into his arms, refusing to look at him. "The storm only makes the dreams worse."

"Worse?" He tilted up her head, brushing the hair from her eyes, a tiny frown creasing his brow. "How often are you having these nightmares?"

117

She didn't have the energy to lie. "They come every night," she confessed.

He stiffened. "*Every night*?"

"Ever since that first incident." She shrugged awkwardly. "You know. With you, in the car."

"Even on the boat?" He searched her face. "All that time you've been having these dreams?"

"I didn't sleep much at night during the trip here," she admitted. "I . . . I was afraid. So I slept during the day, on deck."

"No wonder you're looking so fragile." His mouth compressed. "Why the *hell* didn't you tell me?"

She couldn't meet his eyes. "You weren't there."

"And tonight? When I asked you about the storm?"

"I lied about it not bothering me." She could sense his tension, his disbelief. "I . . . I didn't want you to find out the truth," she tried to explain.

"*Why*?"

"You know why," she told him in a low voice.

It didn't take him long to grasp her meaning. "If you'd told me about the nightmares, I'd have insisted you sleep with me, is that it?"

She nodded. "And I couldn't handle that."

The muscles in his jaw clenched. "In other words, you were willing to put yourself through all this suffering rather than sleep in my bed."

"It wasn't the sleeping I was worried about," she lashed out at him.

"That tears it."

Before she realized what he intended, he stood, lifting her high in his arms. "What are you doing?" she demanded in alarm. "Where are you taking me?"

He headed across the room. "You're so clever. You figure it out."

There was nothing to figure. She knew precisely where he planned to go. "No!" She fought for release, but he didn't even break stride. "I won't sleep with you."

He shouldered past her door. "As you pointed out, sleeping isn't the issue, is it?"

She caught her breath. "You can't mean it, Sebastian. You promised!"

"I promised to give you time. Well, guess what?" His face was dark and stern and totally unrelenting. "Your time's up."

"But... You agreed I could have my own room."

"Then I guess we both lied. So sue me."

A great boom of thunder reverberated through the house, the echo bouncing off the mountains and rolling away across the ocean. Lightning slashed the darkness, white and bitterly intense. Anna shuddered, the fight leached from her. She buried her face in Sebastian's shoulder. Dear heaven, but the storm frightened her, dredging up a hidden terror she couldn't bring herself to face.

Sebastian pushed open the door to his room and crossed to the bed, dropping her onto the mattress. He must have left in a hurry. One pillow lay on the floor, another across the room. And the covers had been kicked into a heap, dangling half on and half off the bed. He saw her eyeing the mess, and a wry smile tugged at his lips.

"Your scream caught me by surprise," he admitted, straightening the bedding.

Rain hammered at the windows and lightning lit the room again. For an instant he stood in bold relief, every detail illuminated. She'd known he had a muscular build, but the sight of him wearing so few clothes hit with stunning impact. He was beautifully shaped, every muscle and sinew sculpted as though by a master. Dark hair covered his chest, darting downward to disappear into low-slung boxers.

She swallowed. "I thought you slept nude."

"I do."

"But you didn't tonight?" Why was she pursuing this? Had she completely lost her mind?

He inclined his head. "I didn't tonight," he agreed.

"Why?" The question was a mere whisper between them. She could only see his silhouette now, his expression buried in the dark. But his posture tensed.

"Because I thought you might need me. And if you did..." He shrugged, weariness underlining his words. "The situation between us is strained enough without my scaring the hell out of you."

Considering how upset she'd been by the storm, she doubted she'd have noticed his nudity. But she didn't dare admit as much to him. Not when he showed such consideration. "It would seem you've won, after all," she told him. "You have me where you originally wanted. So, what do you intend to do now?"

He laughed in genuine amusement, the sound soft and intimate. "Do you really want me to answer that?"

Anna released a silent groan. She hadn't planned for her question to sound as provocative as it did. "I meant—"

"I know what you meant." He approached. "And what I intend is to put you to bed. And then I intend to join you there."

Her pulse quickened. "And if I refuse?"

He picked up the pillow at his feet and tossed it at her. "Lie down."

"Wh-what?"

"You heard me. Lie down."

Her eyes widened in alarm. "Bastian...*please!*"

His footsteps faltered. "Say that again," he ordered.

She stared at him in bewilderment. "Say what?"

"My name. Say my name again."

She licked her lips, stirring uneasily. "Sebastian," she repeated.

"No. That's not what you said. You called me Bastian." He tilted his head to one side. "You're not even aware of it, are you?"

"No," she conceded in a clipped tone.

"You used to shorten my name...before. You were the only one who ever did. And now, when you're frightened, or upset...or aroused, you call to me. You call to me like you used to." He knelt on the bed beside her. "Lie down, Anna."

She shook her head frantically. "No! Please, Basti—" Her breath caught in her throat and she stared up at him, wide-eyed.

Triumph flashed in his eyes. "You do remember. The memories are there, fighting for release. Let me in, my love. Let me help."

Thunder boomed again, and with a smothered cry of alarm, she covered her ears. He had her in his arms before the echo even died away. His heart beat beneath her ear, steady and strong and she relaxed automatically into his embrace.

"It's all right, sweetheart," he murmured. "I'm here."

"Will it end soon?" It was a foolish question. A question a child would ask. But right then, she didn't care. She just wanted the storm to finally be over.

"They don't last long. They're full of flash and fury, but they blow past in short order." He reached down and snagged the sheet, pulling it up to cover them. Repositioning the pillows, he lay back, tucking her close. "Try and sleep. I won't let anything happen to you."

"I can't," she protested. "Not with the storm."

But her eyes drifted closed even as she spoke. And for the first time in weeks she slept. Truly slept, safe and secure within Sebastian's arms, knowing that he would protect her.

Anna woke to an empty bed.

Afraid that Sebastian might walk in at any minute, she slipped from the mattress and hurried back to her own room. She found a maid there busily removing garments from the closet and dresser.

"Excuse me," Anna said, remembering that Dominique had introduced the young girl as a distant cousin. "Ruby?"

The girl turned with a wide, beaming smile. "'Mornin', Mrs. Kane."

"What are you doing?"

"I be movin' your t'ings to the other room," the girl replied, stacking a pile of blouses on the bed.

Anna stiffened. "What other room?"

"To Mr. Kane's room, mom." She shrugged. "He say better I do it sooner than later."

Anna kept a firm hand on her temper. How dare he? How dare he go behind her back, like a thief in the night, and have her things removed? Well, two could play that game. She'd tell Ruby to put everything right back again. She started to speak, then hesitated, realizing her argument was with Sebastian, not with Ruby. Nor did she dare countermand his orders, not with an innocent caught in the middle.

Ruby looked at her curiously. "Be there anyt'ing else, mom?"

"No, thank you," Anna managed to say. "I appreciate your help."

Grabbing a pair of jeans, a cotton blouse and undergarments from the pile on the bed, she hurried into the bathroom. When she emerged ten minutes later, showered and changed, Ruby had disappeared . . . along with all the clothes on the bed.

She eventually located Sebastian in the dining room. At her appearance, he poured her a cup of coffee, adding cream and a smidgen of sugar. That he knew how she liked it, came as another disturbing reminder of all that lay unspoken—and unremembered—between them.

"I told Dominique not to bother serving breakfast," he announced without preamble. "There's a café in the village that offers a selection of pastries. You always had a fondness for their cinnamon rolls. After we finish our coffee, I'd like to drive there. I also thought you might enjoy walking through the markets afterward."

"Fine." She accepted the coffee. "Though right now I'm more interested in discussing why you had Ruby move my things to your room."

He lifted an eyebrow. "You have a problem with that?"

Her cup clattered in the saucer. "Of course I have a problem with it! You agreed to separate rooms until I recovered my memory."

"After last night, that went by the wayside." He took a long swallow of coffee, asking pointedly, "How did you sleep?"

A flush burned her cheeks. She'd slept with all the depth and abandonment of an infant. She'd woken once during the night, only to discover herself wrapped in his arms. She'd been half lying on him, her head cradled securely against his shoulder, her hand buried in the thick thatch of hair spanning his chest. She'd considered moving away, slipping to the far side of the bed.

But she hadn't.

Instead, she'd closed her eyes and pressed her mouth to his chest in a brief caress. And she'd allowed the dreams to come—sweet, gentle dreams of love and light and laughter. Dreams that were far from the dark, foreboding shadows.

She met Sebastian's eyes. "I slept well enough," she admitted cautiously. "But—"

"Then that ends the discussion. You stay in my bed, with me." His gaze swept her face. "And maybe you'll lose that delicate look. Just one decent night's rest has already done you a world of good."

She lifted an eyebrow. "Then you'll let me sleep?" she asked pointedly.

He gave her a dry smile. "Yes. I'll let you sleep." He finished his coffee and stood. "Are you ready to go?"

She wasn't. Nor was she ready for the discussion to end. But short of starting an argument she would undoubtedly lose, there didn't seem to be anything she could do about it. Draining the last of her coffee, she followed him to the Jeep.

To her amazement everything looked just as it had the day before. Butterflies fluttered peacefully among the flowers, hummingbirds dove in and out of the bougainvillea and birds chased each other through the orchid-draped canopy of the trees. She shook her head, marveling at how little impact there had been from the storm.

"I don't understand," she said to Sebastian. "Last night it sounded like a hurricane. This morning it's as tranquil and lush as ever."

He glanced at her, amused. "A hurricane? Last night was just a gentle blow, my sweet. The vegetation is well-accustomed to the wind and rain. To survive, it either bends..." He shrugged. "Or it breaks."

Starting the Jeep, he headed in the opposite direction from the lagoon, the road he took every bit as perilous. Once again, they plunged into the forest, the air rich with the scent of yellow genip blossoms.

The path climbed along the side of the mountain before turning sharply and disappearing into a narrow tunnel, hewn by nature and not readily apparent from either the fortress or the village. On the far side, he stopped. The mountain fell sharply away, and spread below them she could see the village. In between, terraced fields marched up the hillside toward them, overflowing with well-tended crops.

"What are those orchards?" she questioned, pointing further out.

"Banana, nutmeg and citrus." He gazed out at the ripe, green fields in satisfaction. "We also grow cinnamon and sugarcane."

"What more could one ask?" she murmured.

He shot her a strange look. "When you find out, you'll have to tell me," he stated cryptically. "Because I don't know what it could be."

She gazed at him, curious. "And you think I do?"

He shrugged. "There must have been something." Before she could question him further, he shifted into gear and set the Jeep in motion. When they hit the flats at the base of the mountain, he gestured toward a road that split off at a perpendicular angle. "The airfield and my offices are that way. We'll tour those later."

They arrived at the village soon after and the next several hours were sheer delight. They sat outside a busy café that proved to be a local hangout. Mothers with their children came for the thick black coffee, fresh fruit juices and hot-from-the-oven sweet rolls. Everyone greeted her and Sebastian by name and Anna quickly realized that they behaved as if they were a gigantic extended family.

Once she and Sebastian had finished eating, they wandered down toward the harbor. Anna stood for a long time, gazing at the boats jammed around the wharf. "I hadn't expected there to be so many," she commented.

"It's not normally this crowded, but today's market day. Most of these boats are from off-island."

She glanced at him curiously. "I thought you said getting past the reef was difficult."

"It is. See the fishing pirogues?" He pointed to a number of dugouts poised by the mouth of the harbor. "On market day they wait there to greet unfamiliar boats. For a modest fee, they'll escort the visitors safely through the reefs."

She grinned. "And if the visitors don't pay enough?"

He shrugged. "As the islanders are fond of saying, 'What is to be is what is.'"

"Is that like the expression *que sera sera*?"

"You got it. They're on their own and what happens happens. It's in the hands of fate."

Eventually they ended up on the main street, the teeming walkway lined with baskets of produce, fish, lobsters and crab, the merchants and customers chattering in a language similar to French, though with a difference Anna couldn't quite place. They paused by two youths playing an aggressive game of dominoes, but Sebastian drew her away when the shouting turned into a shoving match.

Further along the street, those with a more artistic bent displayed their crafts—paintings, shell and bamboo jewelry and grass rugs. As she walked, children raced up to her, festooning her with necklaces and bracelets they'd made.

"Don't refuse," Sebastian murmured in an aside, when she attempted to protest. "It's their way of welcoming your return."

"What are they saying?" she asked, noticing that a coin found its way into every tiny hand as Sebastian thanked each child personally. "Is it French?"

"It's a French patois mixed with a local slang. They're calling you their good luck lady. They feel that since you first came to the island good fortune has made its home here, as well."

She didn't know what to say, deeply moved by his explanation. So she smiled and exclaimed over each and every piece, sliding the gifts onto her arm or around her neck as though they were the Crown Jewels. Though to her they were far more valuable.

They passed the rest of the day in leisurely exploration of all the village had to offer. They lunched on *kalaloo*, a rich, spicy stew, thick with fish and crab and pork. And they drank passion fruit tea topped with a sliver of sugarcane. Sebastian bought her a straw hat to keep the sun off her face, and held her hand as though it were the most natural gesture in the world. And they spoke to everyone, the hours slipping swiftly by.

The sun was waning in the sky when Sebastian finally suggested they leave. "Would you like to see the island from the air?" he asked. "This would be a perfect time."

She nodded eagerly. "That sounds wonderful."

The drive to the airstrip took little time. Several modern buildings were clustered at one end, tucked close beneath the shadow of the mountain. "The majority of the design work for the planes I build is done on computer in those buildings," he explained, pointing. "I can enter the specs and the computer will do a 3-D mock-up of the plane." He glanced at her. "You worked there for a while. Do you remember?"

She stared intently before shaking her head. "It doesn't look familiar, I'm afraid."

"Don't worry about it."

He parked close to the airstrip and she climbed out of the Jeep, staring at the sleek white craft waiting on the runway, feeling vaguely repelled. "Sebastian . . ."

"Is something wrong?"

Anna hesitated, then shook her head. "I . . . I guess not."

She crossed the tarmac, but with each step she grew more and more uncertain, more and more nervous. She hung back as he unlatched the door and folded down the steps. Stepping aside, he held out his hand and she slowly approached the aircraft. Her mouth was bone-dry, her stomach in knots. She glanced at her hands, amazed to discover that they shook. Reluctantly, she looked back at the plane. The doorway gaped in front of her like a ravenous maw, the steps a shiny, silver tongue waiting to swallow her whole.

"Anna?"

She barely heard him. She put her hand on the smooth, fiberglass skin of the craft and then jerked back as though bitten. "No!" The word escaped in a breathless gasp. "No, no, no!"

"Anna! What the hell is wrong?"

She couldn't explain. She simply turned and ran. He caught her before she'd gone more than ten feet, grabbing her shoulders and spinning her around.

"Let me go!" she shrieked, striking out at him, struggling wildly in his hold. "I won't go in there. I won't! You can't make me!" One of her necklaces broke and shells spilled to the pavement, shattering at her feet.

"Stop it!" He gave her a quick shake. "Anna, you don't have to go near the plane if you don't want to. Calm down. Tell me what's wrong."

She went totally still. "I'm afraid," she whispered. "I'm afraid."

"Of the plane?"

"Yes." She stared up at him, searching his face, fury mingled with disbelief replacing her fear.

"You did that on purpose didn't you?"

A frown creased his brow. "Did what?"

She ripped free of his hold. "You knew, didn't you? How could you? How could you do that to me?"

"Anna—"

She evaded his grasp. "No! Don't touch me! Don't come near me, you bastard. You knew I was afraid of planes, didn't you? *Didn't you*?"

The shaking started then and, ignoring her frantic struggles, he swept her into his arms, carrying her in swift, rapid strides to the Jeep. He deposited her gently in her seat and rummaged in the back. Pulling out a flask, he unscrewed the stopper.

"Here, drink this," he ordered, holding it to her lips.

"No, I—"

"Don't argue! Drink it."

The fight went out of her and she took a deep swallow, gasping as the raw spirits bit at the back of her throat. "What is that?" she demanded once she could speak again.

"You happen to be choking on one of the finest twenty-year-old rums available anywhere."

She lifted an eyebrow. "And you just happen to keep this fine, vintage rum in a flask in your Jeep?"

He nodded gravely. "For medicinal purposes only, you understand."

"Of course," she replied with equal gravity. "Like when your wife has a panic attack?"

He tilted his head to one side. "You know, I think that's the first time since the accident that you've referred to yourself as my wife." He sealed the flask. "Are you all right now?"

"Just wonderful," she claimed, gripping her hands together.

She turned her head so she wouldn't have to look at the plane and removed the necklaces and bracelets, placing them carefully on the dash. She could feel his gaze on her, and felt the return of her tension along with a hot, blinding wrath. She bit down on her lip, struggling to control it.

"I didn't know, Anna," he began. "I swear I had no idea you were afraid of planes . . . of flying."

She glared at him, her fury as cutting as a bitter, arctic wind. "Don't lie to me! I worked for you, was married to you. Flying is your business. How could you not know?"

"Why the hell would I do such a thing?"

She twisted in her seat. "To test me. It's one more way to discover whether or not I've *really* lost my memory. How could you be so cruel?"

"Is that what you think?" Anger swept across his face. "You think I'd do such a thing, put you through such a fright?" He didn't wait for an answer. He circled the Jeep and climbed in behind the steering wheel. "Fasten your seat belt."

"Where are we going?"

"I said, fasten your seat belt. We're going for a ride."

"We haven't finished this discussion."

He turned on her, his eyes almost black with the strength of his rage. "You're right. We haven't finished this conversation. Not by a long shot. But we will. Count on it. We will."

He started the Jeep with a roar, fishtailing the rear wheels in the sand. Heading up the mountain, he practically attacked the road. Just after the tunnel, he veered onto a rough, overgrown track that climbed steeply, the sharp, hairpin switchbacks seeming to continue forever. After a short climb, he slewed into a narrow turnout and switched off the engine.

Reaching into the glove compartment, he pulled out a flashlight and tucked it into his pocket. "Come on. We walk from here," he said, and vaulted out of his seat.

She followed more reluctantly. "Where are we going?"

"You'll see." He lead the way up a rocky path. A boulder blocked the trail, but he simply held out his hand. "Grab on to me," he instructed, helping her around the obstruction.

It didn't take long to realize that he was headed for the very top of the mountain. Up a final incline, she was amazed to see that a passage was cut right through the peak. The hollowed section was tall enough that Sebastian didn't have to duck, and wide enough for the two of them to stand side by side.

"This is Eternity's Keyhole," Sebastian informed her. "As far as we're aware, it's a natural formation."

"It's named for the shape of the tunnel?"

"Yes." He gestured for her to join him inside the passage. "Now watch."

She stood in front of him, framed by the stone keyhole, staring out at a flame-dipped sun as it slowly plunged into the blue Caribbean waters. Never had she seen such colors. It was as though nature had bestowed its blessing on the passing of another day, bidding farewell with all the shades and tints within its spectrum. The softest corals, deepest roses, most brilliant violets all painted a momentary path across the sky.

"It's so beautiful," she said, scarcely daring to breathe.

"Now turn around."

She swiveled, staring out at the opposite side of the island into a dark, ebony sea. A moment later a splash of white shot across the blackness of the ocean. And then the moon tipped over the horizon, turning the water to molten silver.

Sebastian stood behind her, holding her tight within his arms, her spine pressed against the rigid muscles of his chest and abdomen. At last, he spoke.

"I brought you here because I don't think it's possible to stand here and witness what we just did and be anything less than honest. I wanted you to listen to me. To listen and believe."

She knew exactly what he meant. This wasn't a place for lies. It would be... sacrilegious. "I'm listening."

"I was working in Florida when I hired you. I needed an assistant, a dogsbody. Someone to run my errands, and do my bidding. There were plenty of applicants to choose from. But I took one look at you... and I knew. You were the one I had to hire. It was a mistake, one glimpse of those great golden eyes of yours warned me you'd be nothing but trouble. But I hired you anyway."

She bowed her head. "And was I trouble?"

His laugh was short and self-derisive. "What do you think? You've turned my life upside down from the minute you stepped into it. Anyway... After I hired you we worked together for six months. The first five were out of Florida. And then I brought you here. I offered to fly you in, but you had some vacation days coming and wanted to use them on a cruise of the Caribbean."

"So the two times I came here were by boat?"

"Yes."

She couldn't see him, could only hear his voice, low and dark and husky. And devastatingly candid. She didn't doubt a single word he'd said. "What happened when I got here?" she asked.

"You worked in the office at the airstrip with me. The plane I'd built was a prototype, in pieces more often than together. My crew and I were busy testing it, putting it through its paces, fine-tuning the design. So I never found an occasion to take you up in it. And you rarely came over to watch. I didn't attach much significance to it at the time. But I swear to you, Anna. I didn't know you were afraid of planes or flying. You never said and I never suspected."

She nodded, believing him. "What happened next? Did we fall in love?"

He was silent for a long moment and she didn't think he'd reply. Then, in a raw, brutal voice, he informed her, "I seduced you."

"That's not love. Nor does it answer my question." She swiveled in his arms, searching his expression in the cool, ghostly light of the moon. "You say you seduced me. But we married, didn't we? And if we married, we must have loved each other...right?"

He shut his eyes. "You're asking me something I can't answer."

"*Why*?"

He reached for her, his hands sinking deep into her hair. "Because on our wedding night, you slipped from our bed, stripped the rings from your fingers and tossed them onto the sheets..." He tilted her head and stared straight into her eyes. "And then, my sweet wife, you left me."

CHAPTER EIGHT

TEARS welled up in Anna's eyes. "No," she whispered, shaking her head. "I wouldn't have done that to you. I couldn't have. Not on our wedding night."

"It happened," he stated gravely. "It happened just as I said."

She licked her lips, searching frantically for an explanation. "Why? At least tell me why I left you."

Anger blazed in his eyes. "How the *hell* should I know? You never bothered to say. You walked out of the door and out of my life without a single word of explanation. I didn't even know you'd gone until the police arrived at the hotel a half hour later to tell me there'd been an accident."

The puzzle pieces began to fall into place. She closed her eyes, a horrible numbness gripping her. "Why didn't you tell me this sooner?"

Deep lines slashed across his cheeks. "You'd never have come to *Rochefort* if you'd known," he explained roughly. "And I couldn't risk that. I wanted you here, with me, where we could uncover the problem together."

"You mean here under your control," she retorted with a bitter edge.

He gripped her arms, forcing her to listen . . . to believe. "All I ever wanted was to find out why you left. You never said. And it's been eating at me ever since. Put yourself in my place. What the hell should I have done?''

"I don't know," she admitted. Another question troubled her and she glanced up at him. "Tell me something, Sebastian. Why did you think I was faking amnesia? Why have you been so suspicious?''

"It was possible you were using the amnesia as protection, to avoid answering my questions," he replied. "You were injured. You weren't in any position to run again. If everyone believed you suffered from amnesia, it would have given you the time you needed to heal while avoiding my questions.''

A sudden, shocking thought struck her. "That's why you hired a private detective and insisted on escorts if I left my room," she whispered, horrified. "To make sure I didn't run.''

His hands tightened on her arms. "Damn it, Anna! Don't look at me like that. I was desperate. I didn't know what else to do.'' .

"It didn't occur to you to tell me the truth?''

"It occurred to me," he retorted harshly. "But having your wife run out on your wedding night without a single word didn't inspire a lot of confidence in frank dealings or honesty.''

"But I wasn't faking—not then and not now. You do believe me, don't you?''

"I believe you," he stated without hesitation.

She frowned. "If I left you on our wedding night, perhaps that explains why I was so certain you weren't my husband...and why there weren't any marks from the wedding rings. If we'd only just been married that day and then I left...'' She shrugged. "Perhaps I didn't consider myself truly married.''

"Don't kid yourself, Anna. We were married. And the marriage duly consummated."

Color flared in her cheeks. "I didn't mean to suggest—"

He lifted an eyebrow. "Didn't you? You were my wife, even if it was only for a night." He released her, his gaze locking with hers. "Shall I prove it to you?"

Her eyes widened in alarm. "No! That's not necessary. Sebastian—"

Before she realized what he intended, he flicked open the buttons of her blouse. "You have a mole...here." He grazed the underside of her left breast, pinpointing the exact location through the scrap of peach silk. "And another on the inside of your right thigh."

"Please," she whispered. "Don't do this."

"Don't do what? Don't remind you of how it was?"

She fumbled with the shirt buttons, her hair sweeping forward to cover her burning face. "Don't hurt me any more than you already have. I don't think I can bear it."

"Hurt you?" He swore beneath his breath. "Hurting you is the furthest thing from my mind. I want to know what happened. I want to know why you left me. And the only way that's going to happen is if you remember."

She shook her head, taking a hasty step away from him. "It's gone! The memories are gone."

"They're not gone. They're buried. And I swear to you, I *will* find a way to release them. Whatever I have to do, whatever it takes, I'll find the means of bringing you out of that darkness." His voice reverberated within the tunnel, amplifying his drive, his determination.

"The memories won't be forced!" she protested. "Do you think I haven't tried? Do you think I haven't spent every waking moment racking my brains, fighting for a way to pry the past loose?"

He gripped her shoulders, speaking with a passionate urgency. "Think, damn it. Remember! You're timid about removing your clothes in front of me, and you blush the most delicate shade of pink when I strip down in front of you. You walk with unimaginable grace, like a doe picking its way through the forest. You say my name as though you were tasting a rare treat. And when you look at me, the gold in your eyes is so beautiful, it puts the sun to shame."

"Those are mere words," she objected, not allowing him to see how deeply affected she was by those "mere words." "What about the feelings? I asked you before... Did we love each other? Well?" She stared up at him, pleading for reassurance. "Did we?"

"Love?" He regarded her with a bleakness that nearly broke her heart. "I don't think I believe in that emotion anymore. I don't trust it. I'm not certain I ever did."

Her gasp was almost inaudible. She blinked rapidly, backing away from him, fighting to keep the anguish from her voice. "I can't live without love," she told him fiercely, wrapping her arms about her waist. "I won't live without it. If that's how you truly feel, you have to let me go."

He shook his head. "Not until I know the truth," he said, rejecting her plea with icy resolution. "Not until you tell me why you left."

"I think you may already know."

His eyes narrowed. "What's that supposed to mean?"

She lifted her chin. "It means that I wouldn't have married you unless I loved you with all my heart. Nor would I have married someone who didn't return that feeling."

His eyes glittered with a skeptical light. "You told me that once before. How can you be so certain?"

"The memories may be gone, but that doesn't change who I am or the principles I hold most dear," she told him softly, with absolute certainty. "You were the one to help me find the pieces of my personality, to put together those pieces so they formed a comfortable whole. Those traits are as much a part of me, as this island is a part of you. And they tell me I'd only marry for love."

"Well, if you loved me as you claim, then why did you leave?" he demanded tautly. "What possible reason could you have had?"

She met his eyes. "Perhaps I uncovered your true feelings a day too late." Her hands clenched at her sides, but she faced him squarely, hanging on to the shreds of her dignity through sheer willpower. "Or should I say... a *night* too late?"

He stilled, his head tilted to one side as though analyzing her words, and she wondered uneasily what she'd said that intrigued him so. She searched his face, but his expression remained hidden beneath the onslaught of dusk.

"We're not ending this marriage until you've regained your memory," he finally announced.

"But—"

"Forget it, Anna. Nothing you can say will change my mind. You're not in any position, mentally or physically, to make such a drastic decision. It wouldn't be fair to either one of us."

"And I don't think remaining in this marriage is fair to either one of us," she flashed back. "Not if there's no love."

He offered a cryptic smile. "Until you remember why you left me, you stay here."

"Regardless of what I want?"

His smile broadened. "You want to stay. You want to know what happened every bit as much as I do."

She shook her head. "No!"

"Liar." He approached, shadows catching in the crags and valleys of his face, sinking into his gray eyes and emphasizing his broad brow and sharp, angled cheekbones. "You requested that we reenact our past and that's precisely what we're going to do. And maybe, just maybe, we can recover what we lost."

"That's impossible," she insisted shortly.

"Is it? Then prove it to me. Prove to me that what we had is gone forever." His hand closed on her hair, brushing it back from the long sweep of her throat. "Show me that you no longer care."

He lowered his head, nuzzling the unprotected joining between neck and shoulder. She groaned, fighting the sensations that burst to life, fighting to conceal the devastation he wrought. He straightened, gazing down at her with silvered, moonlit eyes and she knew then that resisting him would prove futile.

He knew it, too. "Don't look so tragic. The islanders claim that when the sun and the moon lock together within Eternity's Keyhole, your dearest wish will be granted. What's your dearest wish, Anna? Make it now, while I hold you in my arms and take your mouth with mine."

And then he kissed her, teasing her lips apart and slipping inside. She shifted in protest, but all that accomplished was to bring her closer, fit her more securely within his grasp. She could feel him, every burning inch of him from knee to shoulder, pressing against her. It was like a spark falling onto dry tinder.

The flames caught.

Little by little a restlessness sprang to life deep in her loins, growing to an ache, a sharp craving. Desire forced its way to the surface with all the determination of a seedling erupting from fertile soil. Her resistance lost its battle to a desperate need, like winter, in its frigid barrenness, forced to concede to the ripening fullness of spring, flowering with all the power at nature's disposal.

She loved him. Dear heaven, how she loved him.

And in that moment, held in the sweetest of embraces, all she could wish for was his love in return.

The next ten days passed beneath an uneasy truce. To Anna's relief, the nightmares ended, held at bay, she suspected, by her continued presence in Sebastian's bed. To her surprise, he kept his word. Not once did he try and force a more intimate relationship. Instead he seemed determined to tempt her beyond endurance, teasing her with all the sensual pleasures he swore they'd enjoyed in the past.

"That's it, Sebastian!" she protested, leaping to her feet and brushing the coarse black sand from her knees. "I did not run around without clothes, like some modern-day Eve. Don't try and tell me I did, because I don't believe you."

He lifted onto an elbow, his eyes gleaming with laughter. "I'm just trying to help you remember."

She planted her hands on her hips. "You're just trying to help me out of my bathing suit, you mean."

His grin faded, replaced by a hot, intense stare. "That, too," he conceded.

"Well, it's not going to work." It wouldn't...unless he kept looking at her like that. She turned her back on him and moved down the beach a few paces, glancing over her shoulder. "Come up with another plan."

He stood, gathering up their towels. "Another plan, huh? Okay. How about a swim?"

"Sure. Should I get the snorkels and fins?"

"You won't need them for where we're going," he replied rather mysteriously. "Come on."

He held out his hand and left the beach for the shelter of the forest. A narrow, overgrown path led up the hill, past lichen-covered rocks and between broad expanses of thick ferns. Anna glanced up at the cloudless blue sky partially concealed by the bamboo reeds towering overhead, and wiped the perspiration from her brow. The breeze had trouble reaching them through the dense vegetation, making for a hot climb.

"Not much further," Sebastian called over his shoulder.

She could hear the rush of water now and realized they were approaching the river that fed into the lagoon. A heavily laden frangipani, more tree than bush, blocked her way. She pushed past and a cluster of the richly scented blossoms showered down on her, rose-colored petals catching in her hair and blanketing her shoulders. She lifted a hand to brush them away and stopped dead, staring in amazement at the glade.

He'd brought her to Eden.

And for the first time, a haunting feeling of *déjà vu* struck her.

A huge pool occupied most of the rock-strewn glade, fed by a dazzling waterfall. The water was turbulent toward the center, fleeing to escape the tranquil edges and rush onward—past the bottleneck of rocks closing the base of the pool, to tumble down a series of terraced steps in its desperation to join with the lagoon.

Plants graced the glade, their vivid flowers adorning this hidden pocket of paradise. Large lobster-claw heliconia, a blazing streak of tangerine against a vivid green backdrop, bobbed on long, slender stalks, while parakeets fought overhead, dodging in and out of the palms. A low rumbling whir sounded in her ear and she turned to see a tiny iridescent hummingbird hovering curiously at her shoulder, drawn by her cloak of frangipani. It zigzagged around her in brief, darting forays before retreating to more familiar territory.

She glanced at Sebastian, suddenly aware that he'd been watching her reaction, enjoying her amazement and delight. "It's . . . it's incredible," she told him in hushed tones, unwilling to disturb the indolent atmosphere.

"I thought you'd like it."

"Did I . . . before?"

She couldn't help the leading question. Every place they went, every person they met, she'd wait anxiously for a reaction, anticipating a sense of familiarity. And it had never happened . . . until now. Her breath quickened and a tremor of excitement shot through her as she awaited his confirmation. She'd been here before. She knew this place!

"Yes, you liked it here. In fact, it was your favorite spot." He closed the distance between them and, as though unable to resist, combed his fingers through her hair, sifting out the tiny curling frangipani petals. "This was also a very special place for us," he told her quietly. "Don't you feel it?"

Her lips parted and she closed her eyes. Yes! She could feel it, sense it, almost reach out and touch it. The glade came alive with dreamy wisps of memories. A laugh, a passionate silver-eyed glance, a warm, stroking touch, a driving passion. And then, in a brief, explosive flash, an image burst through the blackness like a piercing ray of white light.

"Do you remember something?" Sebastian questioned sharply.

Reluctantly, she opened her eyes, the memories evaporating like mist beneath the hot Caribbean sun. "Yes! I . . . I saw us here. For a minute, anyway."

"What were we doing?"

Warmth touched her cheeks and her eyes darkened. "We were together," she admitted in a low voice. "In a small hollow behind the waterfall."

He grew still, searching her face with razor-sharp intensity. "There is a hollow there. What else do you remember, sweetheart?" he questioned gently.

"The niche was covered with a downy moss, soft and velvety to the touch."

"A natural bed," Sebastian said, slipping her into his arms. "A bed we shared."

"Yes." Her response was barely more than a whisper. "The waterfall was a solid sheet beside us, nature's curtain, concealing us from the rest of the world. And the water sprayed down, didn't it? It coated us in a fine mist, like a cool sauna. It tickled, but it also—'' She broke off, shivering.

"Aroused?" He cupped her cheek, staring deep into her eyes. "And the sun? Do you remember the sun?"

She nodded. "It shimmered through the waterfall and created diamonds out of the drops of water beading our skin. It was as though we were covered in sparkling jewels. I remember how odd the light seemed. It filled the hollow with a soft green glow and when I looked up..." She struggled to speak, to force the words through the emotions churning within. "A rainbow formed in the mist above us, like a benediction."

"And I took you in my arms..." he prompted in a husky voice. "And then what happened?"

Tears spilled to her cheeks. "You made love to me for the first time."

"Yes. I made you mine. Here. In this place. And afterward?"

She struggled to remember, to push the memory further. But nothing came to her. All she had was that one brief glimpse, a peek into a window at a scene from her past that was so breathtakingly beautiful she found it impossible to believe she could ever have forgotten it.

Her shoulders sagged. "I'm sorry. I don't know what happened next," she confessed.

His hands tightened and for a moment she thought he'd tell her what had occurred. Then his grasp loosened. "It's a start," was all he said. "It would seem we're on the right track. Revisiting old haunts does have a beneficial effect."

She glanced up, curiosity stirring. "Why did you wait so long to bring me to the glade? Considering what happened here, I'd have thought this would have been one of the first places you'd have chosen to visit."

He shook his head. "I wanted to wait until you were stronger, wait until we'd spent more time together."

"Is that the truth?" she questioned skeptically. "Or is it that you were hoping to recreate the moment?"

"If you mean, did I plan to take you behind the waterfall and make love to you, then, yes. Without question."

"You already know my answer to that."

"Shall we visit the hollow and see?"

She drew back. "I don't think so."

"In that case..."

Without warning, he swept her high in the air, carrying her toward the pool. She didn't struggle or protest. There was no point. If he tossed her into the water, he'd join her within seconds. So instead she wrapped her arms around his neck, relishing the feel of his warm, taut skin beneath her hands, appreciating the play of lean muscle and sinew as he moved in long, easy strides. At the water's edge, he lowered her to her feet, his arms locked about her waist. She tilted back her head and gazed up at him for an endless moment.

"What are you thinking?" he questioned tenderly.

A hint of color warmed her cheeks. "I was thinking about how much I'll treasure these moments I've spent with you," she confessed in a low voice. "That if I never recall another second of my past, I'll have this instant to hold on to, this image to call to mind when nothing else is left."

His expression softened. "I can't give you back the past," he murmured. "But I can give you some new memories. Will that do?"

"I'd like that." A breeze stirred the air, caressing her skin with a suggestion of cool, satiny moisture—a misty condensation so delicate, it was almost indiscernible. "Did you feel it?" she exclaimed.

"The liquid sunshine?" he asked, giving the phenomena its Caribbean name. "I felt it. And if you give me your mouth, my love, we'll savor the taste, as well."

She didn't hesitate. Her hands slipped into his thick, black hair and she lifted on tiptoes to kiss him. It was as though a captivating magic filled the glade, the mystic charm of time and place charging the atmosphere. In her mind's eye she saw again that moment in the hollow.

Sebastian had reared above her, the mark of passion full on his face, his bronzed skin slick and glistening. And she'd arched to meet him, moving with an instinct as old as time. The sensations she'd experienced were unlike anything she'd known before...hot, heavy, driving. She'd called out his name, "Bastian!" And the cry had bounced off their rocky nook and blended with the roar of the waterfall.

She shivered, the past merging with the present.

Sebastian lifted his head and stared down at her. "You will remember," he told her quietly, as though aware of the turbulent path her thoughts had taken. "It will come back to you. And then we'll know what really happened." With that he pulled her into the pool, submerging them in the cool, swirling waters.

And she found herself praying she'd never, ever remember. Because she had the uneasy suspicion that to remember would bring their marriage to a bitter end.

Anna knotted the wrap-around bathing suit skirt at her hip and glanced at Sebastian. He lay stretched on a rock, his face relaxed in sleep. He looked rested, peaceful . . . and unbelievably tough. Silently, she left him, picking her way across the rocks and climbing toward the secret hollow. It took her a while to figure out the best path, but eventually she found a way and slipped behind the screen of water.

It was exactly as she remembered. A velvety carpet of moss caressed her bare feet and the same odd green glow filled the oval-shaped recess. The memories lingered, like whispers from a hazy dream. But they didn't become any sharper or more elaborate as she'd hoped.

Sighing in defeat, she returned the way she'd come. Sebastian continued to sleep and Anna decided to follow the terraced steps down toward the lagoon, to see how far she could go. To her delight, she reached the beach with ease, though she could understand why Sebastian had chosen to enter the glade via the forest—the impact was far greater. And, if he'd hoped to spark her memory, he'd certainly achieved a limited success.

She followed the miniature delta to where it emptied into the sea, glancing at the hard metallic-blue sky in concern. An oppressive sultriness weighted the air and she wondered if it meant they were in for another storm. Lord, she hoped not. A wave surged around her knees, tugging at the cotton skirt and she shuddered. She didn't mind the daily downpours that drenched the island at regular intervals. But she dreaded another experience like her first night on the island.

The roar of an engine interrupted her thoughts and she looked up, astonished to see a boat shoot through the rocky opening to the lagoon. She shaded her eyes. A man with reddish-brown hair piloted the craft and, spotting her, he cut the engine and jumped to his feet, the boat rocking wildly beneath him.

"*Chris!*" he shouted, waving his arm in an urgent signal. "Chris, it's me. Come on! Swim out here."

She took a step into deeper water, staring at him in confusion, aware of a frightening sense of familiarity. "Benjamin?" she whispered, then tested the name, calling out, "Benjamin?"

"Yes! It's me. Hurry, before he comes!"

She stood, vacillating, totally bewildered. He knew her. This . . . Benjamin . . . knew her. And apparently, she knew him, as well. Why else would his name come to her with such ease? But . . . he'd called her Chris, which didn't make a bit of sense. She took another step toward the boat, intent on questioning him, the waves lapping at her thighs.

Footsteps pounded across the sand behind her. With a huge splash, Sebastian sprinted to her side, his hand closing on her wrist in a viselike grip. He yanked her back so he stood, rock-solid and immovable, between her and the boat. His chest heaved from exertion, his bronzed skin glistening with perspiration. For a long minute the two men faced off, glaring at each other across the turquoise waters.

There was no question as to who would win this battle for dominion, for possession. The power emanating from the man at her side was absolute. A vehement curse drifted across the water and the speedboat roared to life. Swinging in a tight arc, Benjamin gunned the engine and sped from the lagoon.

Sebastian turned on her. Wrapping an arm around her waist, he hauled her from the water. "Who the hell is that man?" he panted, dumping her to the sand.

She'd never seen him so furious, so out of control. "I don't know!"

"You're lying to me!" He grabbed her by the shoulders, his hands biting into her tender flesh. "I heard you. You said his name. You called him Benjamin."

"I'm not lying!" How could she explain it to him, when she couldn't even explain it to herself? "I don't know him!"

He gritted his teeth, a muscle leaping in his jaw. "Bull! You were wading toward him. He wanted you to swim out to him and you were going to do it. Now, who is he? Tell me, damn it!"

Helplessly, she shook her head, dread tracing an icy path along her spine. "I don't know," she whispered through numb lips, praying he heard the conviction lacing her words. "The name flashed into my mind. But that's all I remember. I swear, that's all that came to me. You have to believe me!"

"More lies?" He thrust her away, as though not trusting himself to touch her any longer. His face was a frightening blank. Only his eyes were alive, the gray burning like white-hot embers. "I don't believe you, Anna. It's all been one, huge lie, hasn't it? You never lost your memory."

She blinked back tears, too proud to allow them to fall. "I did . . . I have!"

"It was all some sort of con job, wasn't it? And this Benjamin is somehow involved."

"No!" Her breath came in great, heaving sobs. "I don't know him, I tell you. I—I mean, I do. I must. But I don't know how. Bastian, please!" she said again. "You have to believe me."

He shook his head. "Not anymore, Anna. Not anymore." Suddenly he froze, his eyes narrowing. "Or... is it Anna? He called you Chris."

It had all happened so quickly, she'd forgotten that particular detail. Until now. She shivered, her confusion growing by the minute. "I don't understand. That's not my name." She gazed up at him in apprehension. "Is it?"

He tilted his head to one side. "No, but it is the name you first uttered—in the hospital after the accident. You called out the name, Chris." He frowned, his brow furrowed in concentration.

To her relief, his intense fury had died, but this frigid remoteness was far worse. She couldn't reach him, couldn't make a dent in his steely control. After a moment he nodded and she could tell that he'd reached a decision. The question was...*what* decision?

"Come on, *wife*. It's time to find out what the hell is going on."

He offered his hand and, bewildered, she stared at it for a long moment. It was such an odd thing for him to do. Considering how furious he'd been, how he'd snatched her from the water and dumped her to the sand, this show of courtesy confused her. Or perhaps this was his subtle way of demonstrating that he didn't intend to manhandle her again. She didn't hesitate another minute. With complete trust, she slipped her hand in his.

He turned and strode with her across the sand toward the Jeep. Anna hastened to climb in as Sebastian started the engine. But instead of charging up the mountain as she'd expected him to do, he flipped on the CB radio and spoke into the mike, barking orders in fast-paced island lingo. He received an immediate response.

"Who did you call? What did you say?" she questioned hesitantly.

"I called the village and told them that we had an intruder—an intruder I want brought in for questioning."

"You can do that?"

He shot her a cool, arrogant look. "It's my island. I can do anything I damn well please."

"And if they succeed in bringing him in?" she asked, dread balling in her stomach. "What then?"

He fixed his gaze on her. His eyes were like diamonds, hard and cold, and glittering with the sparks of a thousand colors. "Then I'll ask him if he's the man who stole you away on our wedding night. I'll ask him if he was the one who drove you off the road and came within a hair of killing you. I'll ask him if he's the bastard who left you there, injured and alone and unconscious, while he escaped from the wreck and disappeared like a thief in the night." He slammed the Jeep into gear, his expression a savage mask. "And if he is, I'm going to take him apart piece by piece."

CHAPTER NINE

ANNA sat in a state of total shock for the entire length of the ride. She didn't know what to think, let alone what to feel. In that one moment, with that single brief statement, Sebastian had turned her world upside down. She'd been aware he'd been keeping something from her, that an unknown chasm still stood between them. But it had never once occurred to her that it could have been another man.

She gripped her hands together, her knuckles bone-white. Was it possible? Could she have left him for this... Benjamin? Silently, she shook her head, not even needing to consider the possibility. No! The love she felt for Sebastian went far too deep, fulfilled her too completely. There had to be another explanation. There had to be!

Sebastian parked the Jeep near Dominique's garden and glanced at her. "I'm sorry, Anna," he said quietly. "I didn't mean for you to find out that way. I'd hoped you'd recover your memory first so we could discuss the situation with clear heads."

She turned to look at him. "You say that as though you still believe I have amnesia," she challenged. "Which is it, Sebastian? Am I telling the truth or am I a liar? Have I lost my memory or not? You can't have it both ways."

He swore beneath his breath, glaring out through the front windscreen. "I don't know what to believe anymore. But I will get some answers, you can count on it.''

"And you think this Benjamin can provide those answers?''

"Yes." As though unable to resist, he tucked a lock of hair behind her ear. "Go on in and shower," he ordered gently. "I suspect our...guest will arrive soon. And I want you there when he does.''

She wished she could say something that would convince him of her innocence. But there wasn't anything to say. She didn't know the truth, any more than he did. Without another word, she slipped from the Jeep and fled through the garden to the side door.

Reaching their room, she stripped off her bathing suit and skirt and stepped beneath the shower. She stayed there for as long as she dared, wishing the cool water could rinse away heartache as easily as it did the brine from the ocean. At last, she shut off the tap and toweled herself dry. She dressed quickly in a gold shirtdress and had just finished pulling her damp hair back in a simple French braid when Dominique rushed into the room.

"We gotta heap o' tribulation," the housekeeper announced, planting her hands on her hips. "You best come quick, mom, befo' Mr. Sebastian does kill that bad mon."

Anna didn't hesitate. She raced from the room and hurried downstairs. Loud voices emanated from the study and she pushed open the door, stepping inside. The two men faced each other. Benjamin rocked on the balls of his feet, his hands clenched, his face beet-red. He sported a black eye. Clearly, he hadn't come of his own free will.

Sebastian stood with a hip resting against his desk, his arms folded, his expression nonchalant. He looked like a sleek, black panther, beautiful and relaxed, resting lazily in the warm sun. But she noticed the tense set of his shoulders and the pulse throbbing in his temple, and realized he was far from relaxed.

"Come on in, Anna," Sebastian said, not taking his eyes from their "guest." "Let me introduce you. Anna Kane, this is Benjamin Samuel. He claims the two of you are old friends."

Her eyes widened. "Samuel?" she repeated, instantly making the connection. She shot a stunned look at Sebastian. "The Samuel who's suing you?"

"The very same."

"Chris, for heaven's sake," Benjamin interrupted furiously. "Tell that bastard how you really feel about him and let's get the hell out of here!"

She shook her head, moving closer to Sebastian. "I'm not going anywhere with you. And how do you know me?" she demanded. "Why are you calling me Chris?"

Bewilderment clouded his eyes. "What are you talking about? Chris is your name. Chris Bishop. And we're..." He glanced uneasily at Sebastian. "We're...old friends."

"I don't remember you," she stated coolly.

He stared, dumbfounded. "How could you not remember? We've known each other for years."

"The accident left her with amnesia," Sebastian explained, straightening from his lounging position. And in that instant it became clear that the lazy cat had turned into a vicious predator. "You do remember the accident, don't you? The one where you were driving well in excess of the speed limit in the middle of a violent storm. The one where you ran the car off the road, tumbling it over and over until it wasn't even recognizable as a vehicle anymore. The accident you ran from while your... *friend*... nearly bled to death.''

Benjamin backed away, holding up his hand. ''I went for help. I did! I walked for miles, but I lost my way. By the time I found a phone the accident had already been called in. I didn't see any point in returning.'' He looked at Anna, as though for support. ''You understand, don't you?''

Anna covered her mouth with her hand and turned instinctively toward Sebastian, needing his strength, his comfort. He didn't hesitate, but took her into his arms. The questions came rapid-fire after that.

''What was she doing in the car?'' Sebastian demanded.

''She was leaving you,'' Benjamin claimed with brutal disregard.

''Why?''

''She'd decided marrying you was a mistake and called, begging me to come and get her before you discovered the truth about us.''

Sebastian's eyes narrowed. ''And what truth is that?''

''That she was helping me win my lawsuit.''

Anna listened in dawning horror, but Sebastian didn't react or comment. It was as though he'd closed himself off, encased his emotions in ice. ''You say you're friends. The relationship between you is close?''

''You could say that,'' Benjamin confirmed with a mocking smile.

"Were you intimate?" Anna started to protest, but Sebastian's hand tightened, quieting her. "Were you?"

"That's none of your business," Benjamin said with an indignation that didn't quite ring true.

"As her husband, it's very much my business. *Were you intimate?*"

Benjamin hesitated, appearing to debate whether or not he'd answer. "Yes!" he finally said, throwing Anna an apologetic look. "I'm sorry if I've embarrassed you, Chris, but I don't see that I have much choice."

"Don't you?" she whispered.

"Not unless I want another black eye." He glared at Sebastian. "Are you happy now? Chris and I were lovers for a few brief months. But it was years ago. There's no need to bring any of that up now."

Sebastian didn't comment. Did he even care? Anna wondered. Or had so much happened that none of it mattered to him anymore. He might be able to face the truth with equanimity, but she was bitterly ashamed that she could have given herself to such a man as Benjamin Samuel, shared the deepest of intimacies with someone so distasteful. "Why was I with you?" she questioned sharply, refusing to remain silent any longer. "And why was I leaving my husband?"

Benjamin glanced at her, then away. "You were working for me on the sly. And you were leaving him because you were afraid he'd find out about it. I think something must have happened that made you suspect he was on the verge of uncovering the truth."

She stiffened. "I worked for you! Like a...a spy or something?"

"Yeah," he admitted, running a hand through his hair. "I needed someone on the inside of his organization, a mole to help me gather information for my lawsuit. I couldn't get at Kane on my own. He's too rich, too powerful, too insular. But when I heard that he'd lost his PA, I offered you money to apply for the job. There was a bonus if he hired you. Once you were in, I could get all the data I needed."

Anna stared at him, appalled. "And I...I *agreed* to this? To spy for you for money?"

Benjamin shrugged awkwardly. "You're basically a nice person, Chris, don't misunderstand. But you've got your eye on the main chance, just like the rest of us. Of course you agreed to it."

She made a small sound of distress and slipped from Sebastian's arms, crossing to the French doors that opened onto the garden. She wrapped her arms around her waist, divorcing herself from the rest of the proceedings. She couldn't bear it. All those fine words she'd thrown at Sebastian about principles and being true to her personality, about love and faith. They were all lies, wishes versus reality—the sort of person she longed to be, not the person she was.

She bowed her head. How could she live with that? Worse, how could she possibly face Sebastian after learning of her duplicity? He must despise her. And seeing the tenderness die from his eyes, seeing them change from that brilliant silver to that flat, cold pewter, would break her heart.

"What was she supposed to get for you?" Sebastian continued the interrogation. "What were you after?"

"I wanted the engineering data for the Seawolf," Benjamin answered. "And the test pilots' reports."

"For the plane your parents crashed in." It wasn't a question.

"No!" came the vehement response. "Not for the plane they crashed in, for the plane that killed them! Your plane. Your badly designed plane."

Sebastian ignored the slur, his questions continuing, smooth and relentless. "But, Anna...excuse me, Chris, didn't steal the specs."

"Not in time for the court case, no. She couldn't get to them because you stored the data here, on the island."

"And once I brought her to *Rochefort*? Why didn't she grab the information when she had the opportunity?"

"She couldn't get her hands on the computer files and get them off the island undetected. Your marriage proposal changed that. She planned to string out the engagement and then smuggle them to me at her convenience."

"Then why did she leave me the night of the wedding?"

"I...I called the whole thing off," Benjamin claimed. A nervous bluster had entered his voice, and curious, Anna turned around. "I told her to forget it. It was too risky to go back to the island with you, especially since you were beginning to suspect something."

Sebastian's eyes narrowed. "You were so close to attaining your goal, and you called it off? That doesn't make much sense."

Benjamin drew himself up. "Despite what you might think, I do care for her. I didn't mean for that accident to happen, and I'm really sorry she got hurt. Nor did I expect her to marry you. When I found out, well ... Quite frankly, I was shocked that she'd go to such extremes. I hadn't asked her to, that's for sure."

There was the unmistakable ring of truth in his words, and Anna didn't doubt for a minute he believed every word he told them.

"Then why did she marry me?" Sebastian demanded.

"Maybe she thought she could make even more money married to you than she could helping me."

Anna gasped, stunned by the viciousness of the remark. Sebastian didn't care for it, either. His hand closed into a retaliatory fist and for a minute she thought he'd resort to the most primitive response possible for silencing an adversary. She didn't know whether to be relieved or disappointed when a knock interrupted him.

Dominique's burly husband entered. "The room's ready," he announced. "You done with him?" He jerked his head in Samuel's direction.

"Yes, Joseph. We're quite finished." Sebastian studied Benjamin, his voice soft and more of a threat than Anna had ever heard before. "Joseph is going to show you to your room for the evening. If you cause any trouble, you'll have more than a black eye to worry about. Is that clear?"

"Wait a minute!" Benjamin protested. "I want to leave the island. I told you everything I know. You can't hold me here against my will!"

Sebastian released a short, harsh laugh. "Yes, I can. But that's not why you're staying. There's a storm moving in and it's not safe to leave right now. First thing in the morning, I'll arrange for you to be transported off the island."

The explanation seemed to mollify him. "And Chris?"

"That's none of your concern," came the wintry response.

"But—" Joseph dropped a heavy arm on Benjamin's shoulder, propelling him toward the door. And with a helpless look in Anna's direction, he left.

Sebastian glanced at her, an enigmatic expression darkening his eyes. "So... It would seem I married a spy."

She gathered every scrap of fortitude at her disposal and met his gaze. "I'm sorry, Sebastian. I know you have no reason to trust me, but I sincerely regret whatever part I played in this whole business."

"Then you believe him?" he questioned idly. "You're certain you're capable of doing the things he's accused you of?"

She swallowed. "I don't want to believe it. But without proof to the contrary..." She faltered, unable to continue.

"Don't worry about the proof. By tomorrow we'll have all we need."

"Tomorrow?" she questioned in alarm. "What happens then?"

"I hear from the detective I hired after your accident. Now that he has more information to go on, he'll be in a position to confirm...or deny Benjamin's story."

"And when he does?"

His mouth tightened, his scar standing out in sharp relief. "Then I'll know how much trouble my wife has gotten herself into."

She swallowed. "And in the meantime?"

His eyes glittered darkly. "In the meantime, we wait."

The storm woke her, sending her fleeing back to Sebastian's bed.

"I wondered how long it would take you," he commented the minute the door burst open.

"I thought, considering what Benjamin had said about me, that sleeping in the other room was more considerate," she began a trifle incoherently. Thunder boomed overhead, cutting her off, and she flew across the room. "But I've changed my mind."

"Well, what are you waiting for?" He shifted in the bed. "Come on."

She didn't need a second invitation. She stumbled in her haste to join him, jabbing him in the stomach with her elbow. To her relief, he didn't take offense. Nor did she have to ask to be held. The minute she'd settled onto the mattress, he wrapped her in his arms.

It felt like she'd come home.

"I shouldn't be here," she murmured, daring to slip her hand into the thick hair covering his chest. But she was glad she had.

"Because of Benjamin?"

"Yes."

"Because he claimed you and he were lovers?"

She bit down on her lip and nodded, finding his frankness difficult to match.

Sebastian released his breath in a long sigh. Then he rolled onto his side, facing her. "There's something I haven't told you," he said, cupping her cheek and stroking the curved sweep of her jaw. "Something you should know."

Her laugh sounded shaky. "If it's more bad news, I'd rather not hear."

"It's not bad." He hesitated, then said, "He lied to you, Anna. Benjamin lied. You were never his lover. You couldn't have been. When I made love to you in the hollow behind the waterfall, you were a virgin."

She froze. "That flash of memory I have of us together...?"

"Wasn't just the first time we made love," he said tenderly. "It was also the first time you were with a man."

"Do you mean that?" she whispered, tears of gratitude leaping to her eyes. "You're not just saying that?"

"It's the truth. And after we made love, I proposed to you. He can't know you very well if he thought you were prone to affairs. So the question remains... who the hell is he to you?"

"I don't want to think about it," she told him tautly. "I don't want to think about *him*."

His voice deepened. "Then what do you want to think about?"

"I want..." she began, then shook her head. "But that's not possible."

"What is it, my love? What do you want?"

"I wish... I wish I could remember how we were together. Before the accident, I mean," she whispered the aching confession. "I have no memories, except for that brief flash of what we shared in the glade. But the weeks I lived with you on the island, your proposal, the other times we... we made love, and that one night I spent as your wife have all been taken from me. I can't remember. And I want to. More than anything in the world I want to remember."

There was a long moment of silence. And then he said, "We could change that. We created new memories once before. We could again."

She literally stopped breathing. If Benjamin was to be believed, she'd committed a terrible betrayal. In the morning, when Sebastian heard from the detective, he'd discover the full extent of her crimes. And he'd undoubtedly put her off the island, end their relationship. More than anything, she wanted a single memory she could take with her. One night of rapture to sustain her through the dark days ahead.

Without a word, she left the bed. She heard his soft curse, and smiled, understanding the reason for it. Except for the occasional flash of lightning, the room remained pitch black, and as she unfastened the row of pearl buttons lining the bodice of her nightgown, she was grateful for the concealing darkness. *You're timid about removing your clothes in front of me . . .* His words crept into her mind and taking a deep breath, she shoved the straps from her shoulders, allowing the thin cotton to pool at her feet.

"Anna, what—"

Lightning bleached the sky.

The breath hissed from his lungs. "Dear, God," he whispered hoarsely. He didn't move and after an eternity his voice came to her in the darkness, raw and aching and thick with need. "You better mean this, Anna. Because once I touch you, there is nothing on earth that will get me to stop."

"I don't want you to stop. I want you to make love to me for the first time...again," she pleaded. "Make me your wife, even if it's just for this one night."

He didn't need a second bidding. He came off the bed, stripping his shorts in one easy move. Lightning flared again and she could see the extent of his desire. She trembled and his brows drew together in concern.

"Don't be afraid," he told her gently. "I won't hurt you."

She lifted her gaze, looking at him with stunning directness. "It's not fear."

Comprehension dawned and he reached for her. "Then let me show you how good it is between us."

Slowly, with infinite care, he lowered his head and captured her mouth, drinking with a passionate thirst. He cupped her bottom, drawing her close, introducing her to a deeper physical intimacy with caution and restraint, allowing her to grow accustomed to the feel of him, to the undeniably masculine shape of his body.

And she realized, with a dawning sense of wonder, that he knew her, knew her thoroughly. He knew her every want and need, thought and desire almost before she was aware of them herself. There was a sureness to his touch, a level of familiarity, as though he were reacquainting himself with a well-loved treasure rather than exploring new territory.

She let him touch her where he willed, opening herself to him without hesitation or restraint. And she discovered that by accepting each and every new intimacy, she was rewarded by ecstasies beyond any she'd ever imagined. He found the tiny mole on the underside of her breast, tasted it, took it into his mouth, while his hand traced her inner thigh to find its mate. Her legs gave out, and he fell with her to the bed, positioning her for his possession.

What came next was so perfect, so shattering, so intensely elemental that it rivaled the ferocity of the storm beating at their windows. It caught her totally unaware. She wasn't prepared for the force of her desire, for the tempest of sensation that broke over her as he took her, showed her all she'd dared to forget.

Afterward, she lay gasping, fighting for breath, fighting for sanity. "Bastian! Is this how it was the first time? Was it like this in the glade?"

He lifted his head, his heart pounding against hers. "Was it this special? This wild?"

"Yes." She gazed at him uncertainly. "Was it?"

"Every bit as much," he reassured. "And yet this time there's also the richness, the deeper texture that comes with experience and familiarity."

A frightening realization broke over her. One night wasn't enough. She wanted more. She wanted that experience and familiarity to continue—to go on and on for the rest of her life. Exhaustion gripped her, and sensing it, he gathered her close.

She snuggled, safe in his arms, the final shattering moments of their passion still rippling through her. Slowly, she drifted off to sleep. And she began to dream . . . to remember. It was as though with that single act of love the shadowy curtain concealing her past had shredded, the darkness dissipating, allowing the memories to escape. And they came, the memories came, gently, relentlessly, unfolding in her dreams . . .

She dreamt. . . .

Lightning flashed across the midnight sky, igniting the hotel bedroom with a momentary brilliance. Anna turned her head and glanced at Sebastian. He slept deeply, fully, his arm wrapped with possessive strength about her waist, the taut, strong lines of his face momentarily relaxed.

It was time.

She inched from his grasp, wincing as well-tested muscles protested the movement. For a moment, his grip tightened, threatening to impede her escape. Then his fingers relaxed, sliding from her naked hip. She didn't lose another minute, but dressed with silent speed. Snatching up her purse, she reached for the doorknob and froze. One final, terrible obligation remained.

She hesitated, not daring to return to the bed, afraid if she did she'd never find the strength to leave. Instead she tugged the precious wedding rings from her finger and pressed them to her lips before tossing them gently toward her pillow. Thunder growled in the distance and another flash of lightning blazed from the uncurtained windows, catching on the rings as they tumbled over and over through the air. She closed her eyes, struggling to hold the tears at bay.

She was late. She had to go.

Still, she couldn't seem to move. She stood there, staring at her slumbering husband, striving to imprint a lifetime of memories, to capture this moment for the dark days ahead. Covering her mouth with a trembling hand, she spun around and silently slipped from the room.

The wait for the elevator seemed interminable and the ping announcing its arrival echoed with shrill resonance through the empty corridor. Stepping into the car, she slammed her palm repeatedly against the button for the lobby until the doors slid closed and the elevator began its descent. The ride took forever. At long last, the doors parted, opening the way to her escape. She fought the instinct urging her to run. Instead, she walked leisurely across the marble foyer, feeling the curious gazes of the desk employees every step of the way.

Even in the wee hours of the morning, a doorman stood on duty. "Would you like a cab, Miss?" he questioned as he opened the door.

She shook her head. "I'm being met, thank you," she said, instantly regretting the admission. But it was too late to call back the words. So now Sebastian would learn she hadn't left alone. Well, he'd learn soon enough once he received her letter.

From across the street a car leapt to life, racing into the hotel drive and sliding to a halt in front of her. Benjamin thrust open the driver's door, hovering half in and half out of the dark sedan. Huge drops of rain splattered his hair and shoulders, runneling down the taut planes of his face.

"You're late," he shouted. "Come on!"

She stepped from the curb and opened the door. But she didn't get in. Something stopped her, a touch of regret, of longing, causing her to take a final wistful look back. Then the heavens opened, drenching her and she hurriedly climbed into the car. With a screech of tires, they roared away from the hotel.

"Did you get it?" Benjamin demanded.

She shook her head. "No."

"What do you mean, no?" he shouted, skidding into a turn.

The rain intensified, coming with such ferocity, she could barely make out the road in front of them. "Benjamin, be careful," she urged. "Slow down."

He ignored her, fury tightening his mouth. He shot around the next corner, faster this time, as though in deliberate defiance. "You were our only hope. How could you do this? You've ruined everything. Everything!"

Tears blurred her eyes. She couldn't deny it. She'd betrayed everyone who'd meant anything to her. "I'm sorry," she whispered brokenly. "But you said you'd given up on the case. You gave me your blessing to pursue a relationship with Sebastian."

"Because I knew you'd be in an even better position to get the computer files! Did you really think I'd drop my suit just because you're stupid enough to fall for the guy?"

"Yes! Or I'd have left him months ago. He's innocent, Benjamin. You're going to have to face the fact that it was a tragic accident. Perhaps a therapist—"

"No! It wasn't pilot error! It was a design flaw." He pounded on the steering wheel. "I warned you what would happen if you didn't get the information. I haven't changed my mind. Don't think I have. I'll tell him who you really were. I'll tell him you're my stepsister."

"Do what you must, Benjamin," she said wearily. "It doesn't matter anymore. I've left him."

"You *what*?"

"You heard. I left him. And I sent a letter explaining everything." Tears spilled down her cheeks and she turned her head so he wouldn't see her anguish. It was too private, too raw. "You have nothing left to hold over me, nothing left to blackmail me with. It's over."

He swore violently. "What the hell are we supposed to do now?"

"Give up." The response came from the heart, filled with both hope and despair.

"Never," Benjamin snarled, stomping on the accelerator in his fury. "I'll never give up until that man pays for murdering our parents. Until he's broken, in jail and destitute, the bast—"

An ear-splitting crack of thunder swallowed the last of his words and lightning streaked wildly across the sky revealing a blind curve just ahead. Anna screamed, knowing Benjamin would never make the turn, that in his fury he'd drive them straight over the edge of the hillside.

For a brief instant the car soared through the air. Crashing to the ground, the doors popped, throwing Benjamin clear before flipping. It tumbled over and over and over, like wedding rings tossed onto a bed, came her final frantic thought. The sickening shriek of ripping metal deafened her, then the pain came, sharp and intense. "Bastian!" she screamed. And at long last, blessed darkness engulfed her.

Anna sat up with a gasp. She remembered. She remembered it all.

CHAPTER TEN

ANNA turned, about to wake Sebastian and tell him she'd remembered everything, until she realized just what that would entail. She hesitated. She needed to think first, consider what she'd say. Silently, she slipped from the bed and dressed, painfully aware she'd played this scene before—on her wedding night, no less. She didn't like it any better now than she had then. Only this time she wouldn't run. This time she'd stay and face the music.

She crept to the kitchen and made herself a cup of coffee. Dawn hadn't quite broken, but a lightness gathered in the air, warning of its approach. Cupping the mug in her hands she wandered through the silent house. Outside Sebastian's study, she paused, drawn by the furtive rustle of papers and the scraping of wood. She pushed open the door. Benjamin sat behind Sebastian's desk, riffling through the drawers.

"What are you doing? Are you insane?" she said with a gasp.

His head jerked up and he glared at her. "If you know what's good for you, you'll get the hell out of here."

"I'm not going anywhere." She closed the door. "Not until we have a talk. Where's Joseph? What have you done to him?"

"I haven't done a thing. He's sound asleep, snoring loud enough to wake the dead. I picked the lock and walked right by him."

"And came down to search Sebastian's desk? Benjamin, please. You have to end this vendetta. Our parents wouldn't have wanted this, not if it destroys you in the process."

He released a short, cynical laugh and tossed the papers to one side. "So you were faking the amnesia. I wondered."

She shook her head, refusing to allow him to anger her. "I wasn't faking. It came back to me last night during the storm. *Everything* came back."

"How convenient. You now remember." He swiveled in the chair, studying her intently. "So what are you going to do about it?"

"I'm going to tell Sebastian the truth."

"She's turned noble, as well," he sneered. "And how do you suppose he'll respond? Forgive you for deceiving him? You're deluding yourself if you think that. Because the truth is, you did take that job in order to spy for me—"

"But not for money! Never for money. I did it because I sincerely believed the Seawolf was at fault for the crash."

"It was!"

She planted her hands on the desk and leaned across toward him. "I saw the files, Benjamin. I read all the reports. There's nothing wrong with the plane."

"You read the reports?" he questioned eagerly. "You know how to access the information?"

"Yes, but—"

He shoved back the chair and stood. "Where is it?" he demanded. "Where does Kane keep his files?"

"Not here. The computers are at the airstrip." She skirted the desk, laying a hand on his arm, pleading with him. "Give it up, Benjamin. Revenge isn't going to change anything. All it's going to do is hurt you, add to your misery. It's not going to bring back your father or my mother.''

"Do you think I don't know that?'' he replied, the anguish clear in his voice. "But I can't let them die in vain. Not without *doing* something."

Tears filled her eyes. "Oh, Benjamin. Don't torture yourself. It's not your fault. You flew that plane the best you knew how. I know the verdict read pilot error. But I don't blame you for the accident, I swear I don't.''

It was the wrong thing to say. His expression hardened and he grabbed her arm. "Come on,'' he said. "We're leaving.''

"I'm not going anywhere with you,'' she protested, twisting in his grasp. "I'm staying here. I have to explain to Sebastian, tell him I have my memory back.''

His hold tightened. "You can explain to him after you help me get those computer files.''

Before she realized what he intended, he unlatched the French doors and pushed her into the garden. "There's a Jeep parked under the breezeway around the corner. We'll take that.''

He ushered her through the garden, ignoring her pleas, her resistance. Morning was moments away and the birds stirred, rehearsing their greetings. A golden pheasant burst from a bed of red ginger lilies and disappeared into the forest. Benjamin seemed oblivious.

"I won't come,'' she told him, digging in her heels. "You can't make me.''

He turned on her, yanking her close. "I'll use force if I must. I don't want to, but I'm out of options here.'' His face bore an unhealthy ashen hue, while his cheekbones were streaked with a mottled red. His hands trembled. But it was the look in his eyes that worried her most, a frantic, hopeless, desperate look that frightened her, warned her of how badly he needed help.

"Come inside with me," she pleaded. "We can talk."

He shook his head. "No. You have to come with me. I must see those computer files."

An idea occurred to her then, a possible way out. "If... if I show them to you, will that be enough? Will that satisfy you?" she attempted to compromise. "You can't take them with you, but you can read through them."

He lowered his gaze, his brow furrowed in thought. "You'll show them all to me?" he questioned, shooting her a sharp look. "You won't hold any out?"

"You can read everything. I promise." She licked her lips. "But there's one more condition."

He eyed her suspiciously. "What?"

"You have to let me drive."

A bitter smile twisted his mouth. "I guess I can't blame you for that." He gestured toward the driver's side of the Jeep. "Be my guest."

She'd pushed him as far as he'd go, she'd get no further concessions. Sliding behind the wheel, she started the engine and released the clutch, heading toward the village. The road was slippery, too slippery for safety. But she didn't dare suggest they turn back. Dawn arrived just as they exited the tunnel and started down the hill toward the airstrip, the sun sweeping across the slopes of the mountain with golden warmth.

It was then that she realized they were being followed, catching the glint of light on metal in the rearview mirror. And she knew, deep in her bones,

that it had to be Sebastian. It wouldn't be long until
he overtook them; he was moving at a fast clip. She
shot a quick glance at Benjamin, wondering if he'd
noticed. She didn't think he had. His full attention
remained focused on the road ahead.

She bit down on her lip, afraid Sebastian must believe the worst, must suspect that she'd left him again,
that she'd schemed with Benjamin from the start, and
that her amnesia was just a devious means to get at
the computer files. Once he learned she'd regained
her memory, he'd be convinced of it.

She forced her attention back to the road, aware
that regrets could come later. For now, she had to
concentrate on her driving. It had become increas-
ingly hazardous, overnight streams appearing as a
result of the storm and cutting across the road in their
mad dash to lower ground. She rounded a sharp curve
and bounced through yet another torrent of water,
horrified when she saw the ground collapsing just after
they passed. Sebastian! He'd never be able to stop in
time! She slammed on the brakes, stalling the engine.

"What the hell are you doing?" Benjamin shouted.

There was no time to explain. Leaping from the
Jeep, she dashed back up the road, hoping to warn
Sebastian before he got to the curve. But she knew,
with a horrifying certainty, that she would be too late.

His car rounded the corner a split second ahead of
her. She saw the instant comprehension that appeared
on his face, the grim set of his features, his desperate
attempt to avoid the collapsed section of road. For a
split section, she thought he'd make it. Then his Jeep
skidded violently and plummeted over the side of the
hill.

"*Bastian*!" she shrieked.

She ran to the edge of the landslide, sobbing beneath her breath, certain she'd be forced to witness his death. She stared in disbelief. Miraculously, the Jeep hadn't flipped, but had rolled down the embankment and crashed into a palm tree at the very edge of the next switchback below. The passenger side had taken the brunt of the impact. Sebastian sat slumped over the steering wheel, unmoving. Benjamin appeared at her side, took one look and grabbed her arm.

"Come on. Hurry. That palm may not hold."

He took the driver's seat, starting the engine and releasing the clutch just as she jumped in. It took mere minutes to travel around the next series of curves, but it seemed like hours. He stopped the car feet from the accident.

To her horror, Sebastian's face was covered in blood. "Head wound," Benjamin announced tersely. "I don't want to move him, but he needs medical attention right away. I'm going to pull in closer and we'll see if we can't shift him to our Jeep."

"But there's no doctor on the island," she told him. "If there's a serious accident Sebastian always flies them to the hospital in San Juan."

Benjamin froze. "In his plane? A Seawolf?"

She clutched her hands together. "Yes. Can you do it? Can you fly it?" It was a lot to ask, an almost unthinkable request to make, but there wasn't anyone else available.

For an endless moment he stared at Sebastian, then he turned and looked at her, a terrible expression filling his eyes. "I'll do it. I'll take him to the hospital...in exchange for the computer files."

"No! You can't mean that! Benjamin, for God's sake, you can't bargain for a man's life."

"I'm not bargaining. You are. Do you want my help, or don't you?"

She didn't have any choice and they both knew it. "I'll hate you for this," she told him, her voice breaking. "If you force me to betray him, I'll hate you for the rest of my life."

"Then hate me," he said callously. "But if you want to save him, you'd better make up your mind. Do you agree or not?"

She closed her eyes, despair filling her heart. *Oh, Sebastian,* she cried silently. *Forgive me.* Then she looked at her stepbrother and gave a tight-lipped nod. "I agree," she whispered. "May heaven help me. I agree."

It took every ounce of willpower to climb into that plane. If it hadn't been for the seriousness of Sebastian's injury she'd never have been able to go through with it. For years afterward, what she remembered most about the flight to Puerto Rico was the acrid scent of terror that filled the aircraft. Benjamin didn't speak a word the whole time, his face gaunt and drawn, his eyes lifeless, the panic kept barely in check. How he managed to fly, she never knew.

The only thing that preserved her sanity through the ordeal, that kept fear from driving her mad, was Sebastian. From the moment she climbed aboard, to the instant they touched down, she never once took her eyes off her husband.

An ambulance waited for them at the airport. And when at long last they wheeled Sebastian into the emergency room, she turned on Benjamin, blocking his access.

"You have what you wanted," she told him with cold bitterness. "Now take your files and go."

"Chris—"

"It's not Christianna anymore," she cut in sharply. "I changed my name at your request when I went to work for Sebastian. Remember? It's just plain Anna now."

He nodded awkwardly. "Okay...Anna. Please, try and understand why I'm doing this."

She drew away. "Oh, I understand. I understand that nothing matters to you anymore except finding a scapegoat. You can't live with the fact that you flew the plane that killed our parents. Well, those computer files aren't going to give you any peace. Go away, Benjamin. I don't want you here." And with that, she turned on her heel and left him.

The wait for the doctor's report was interminable. The whole time she faced the grim certainty that if Sebastian died, a part of her would die, as well. And if he lived, he'd probably hate her for the rest of his life. She'd betrayed him. From the first minute she'd met him, she'd betrayed him. And somehow she doubted he could ever forgive her for that.

The doctor appeared in the doorway and she leapt to her feet. "How...how is he?" she asked.

"He'll be fine, Mrs. Kane. It looked much nastier than it was."

She could have wept in relief. "May...may I see him?"

"Of course, though I should warn you he's been sedated. The nurse will show you to his room. Don't stay too long. He needs his rest."

The nurse led the way down a long corridor and finally pushed open a door. "Ten minutes, Mrs. Kane. There'll be plenty of time to visit tomorrow."

The lights in the room were dim, the afternoon sunshine muted. Though there were two beds, Sebastian was the only occupant. Silently, she approached, gazing down at him. He lay deathly still, a white bandage wrapped around his brow. She lifted a trembling hand to her mouth, closing her eyes in anguish. Is this how he'd felt after her accident? she couldn't help but wonder. Had he experienced this level of despair and panic?

She needed to touch him, to reassure herself that he'd be all right. She glanced toward the closed door, then lowered the railing on one side of the bed and fit herself into the narrow space next to him. She didn't care if they came in and caught her. Nothing mattered, but having these few minutes with him.

"Bastian?" she called softly, wondering if he could hear her, wondering if he slept or if the sedation had rendered him unconscious. He didn't respond. His breathing continued, deep and regular. Tears gathered in her eyes. "Oh, my love, what have I done to you?" she murmured, heartsick. "I've brought nothing but pain and difficulty into your life."

She shifted closer, knowing that if she didn't say the words now, she might never speak them. "I betrayed you, Sebastian," she forced out the confession. "In so many ways. I did work for Benjamin because . . . because he's my brother and he asked for my help. And there's something worse. I . . . I gave him the computer files."

She waited for a response, for him to give some indication that he heard. He didn't move. Tenderly, she swept the hair from his brow, traced his sculpted cheekbones and taut jawline, lingering on the firmly chiseled mouth. How could she have forgotten him, forgotten he was her husband? It seemed impossible. Lifting onto an elbow, she kissed him, softly, sweetly, with gentle passion.

"I love you, Sebastian," she whispered. "I should have said it last night. I wish I had. I wish I'd told you then how much you mean to me. And if all I ever had was a single night as your wife, it would have been worth it." Her voice broke, but she persevered, speaking the words that were in her heart. "It would have been worth it because one night as your wife is worth a lifetime in the arms of any other man."

There was nothing left to be said. She closed her eyes and held him, hoping to give him a small piece of her strength, willing him to recover...to come back to her.

A few minutes later, the nurse poked her head in the door. "I'm sorry, Mrs. Kane," she said regretfully. "It's time."

Anna slipped from the bed and gazed down at Sebastian. "I have to go now, but I'll be back," she told him. "I promise. I'm not running away this time."

Joseph met Anna at the hospital early the next morning. "I'm sorry, Mrs. Kane. Mr. Sebastian, he's not here. He has left."

She stared, stunned. "Left? How could he leave when he's hurt?" she demanded, the questions tumbling free one after the other. "Is he all right? Where did he go? Who authorized it?"

Joseph shrugged. "Mr. Sebastian, he need no authority but his own. But he did make arrangements for your transportation to Florida." He added kindly, "It's by boat."

She shook her head. "No! I have to speak to him. I have to explain...."

Joseph just stood there, his arms folded across his chest. "No, mom. You have to go to Florida."

She opened her mouth to argue again, then closed it, her shoulders sagging in defeat. What was the point? She didn't know where Sebastian had gone, how to get in touch with him. And clearly, Joseph wasn't going to help her. He had his orders—put her on the boat. She looked at him, inclining her head with as much dignity as she could muster.

"Very well. I'll go to Florida. But you can tell Sebastian for me that this isn't over. Not by a long shot."

Joseph grinned. "Yes, mom. I tell him dat for you."

The next day and a half inched by. She ran the gambit of emotions between hope and despondency. By the time she reached Florida, despondency had won. He hated her. He despised her. That's why he'd refused to see her in Puerto Rico. She'd betrayed him, and he'd never forgive her. And why should he? She couldn't help the thought. She'd done nothing to earn his forgiveness, his understanding.

And yet... The one tiny light in the midst of her desperation was realizing that even when he'd thought the worst of her, even when he'd thought she'd left him for another man, that she'd been a spy within his organization, he'd still kept her at his side. He'd made love to her with a depth and passion that couldn't be feigned. And he'd tried, with amazing patience and determination, to get to the truth. Surely it meant he still had feelings for her?

She groaned. Feelings she'd done everything within her power to destroy.

A car met her in Florida. "I have orders to deliver you to the *Island Oasis*," the driver informed her, opening the door to the limo.

She stared in shock. "No. There must be some mistake. That's—" That's where they'd spent their honeymoon night. He couldn't be so cruel. He couldn't!

"Mr. Kane left very explicit orders. Deliver you to the *Island Oasis*."

Like some forgotten parcel? Her mouth tightened. "And if I refuse to go with you?"

The driver shifted uncomfortably. "If you refuse, I'm to tell you that Mr. Kane will have you and a Mr. Benjamin Samuel arrested for theft." He cleared his throat, offering sympathetically, "I suggest you come, Miss. He looked quite serious."

Once again she'd been left with no other option. Nodding, she stepped into the limo and made herself comfortable. An hour later they arrived at the hotel. It took every ounce of courage to step from the car and enter the lobby, not in the least surprised to discover she was expected. In two minutes she'd been checked in and accompanied to the elevators.

"If you'd give me the key," she told the youthful porter, "I can find my own way."

He turned beet red. "I've been asked to escort you... personally."

The temptation to ask "And if I refuse...?" was almost too much to resist. But one look at the poor boy's expression ensured her silence. "Thank you," she said lightly. "I appreciate your thoroughness."

He grinned in relief. "Just doing my job."

Of course, it was the same room as last time, the Honeymoon Suite. At first she felt relief that Sebastian wasn't waiting for her. It gave her time to freshen up. But after an hour, with the tension building minute by minute, she just wished he'd arrive and get it over with. When the door finally opened, she started badly, her nerves stretched to their limits.

He looked impossibly remote, dressed in a business suit and tie. He didn't say anything at first, not a word of greeting, not even a word of accusation. He simply stood for a long moment and stared at her. Then he shut the door.

A stark white bandage covered a corner of his brow, drawing her gaze. "Are you all right?" she asked hesitantly.

"Just one more scar to compliment all the others," he said in a grave voice.

She couldn't tell whether he meant it humorously or not. "I'm sorry," she said awkwardly. "I tried to warn you."

"I know. Thank you for that." He led the way into the living room, tossing a pair of envelopes onto the brocade sofa. He removed his suit jacket and stripped off his tie, working at the buttons constricting his throat. His shirt gaped, revealing the dark hair matting his chest, and she was helpless to look away. He nodded toward the envelopes. "Those are for you."

She moistened her lips. "What . . . what are they?"

"One's a letter from your stepbrother. A letter of apology, I should imagine."

Her gaze flashed to his. "You know?" she whispered. "You know Benjamin's my brother?"

He lifted an eyebrow. "You told me in the hospital, remember?"

"Well...yes," she said, disconcerted. "But I didn't realize you'd heard me."

He met her eyes with stunning directness. "I heard every word you said."

The breath stopped in her throat. "Every word?" she repeated, disillusionment edging her voice. "Then why didn't you say anything at the time? Why did you let me walk away without offering a single comment in reply?"

His mouth twisted. "If you recall, I wasn't in any position to comment. And even if I had been, I had no intention of discussing our life history from a hospital bed, with doctors and nurses tromping in and out every five minutes. Later that night, Benjamin stopped by and I had to deal with him before I could discuss your...confession. He was in pretty bad shape."

She could barely take it in. "Benjamin came to the hospital? What did he tell you?"

"The truth, for a change. Or rather, a slightly more accurate version of his previous statement."

"I don't suppose you could be more specific?" she asked warily.

He crossed to the window. Dazzling bright sunshine outlined his features in a blaze of gold. "He said he didn't pay you to apply for the job as my PA, merely asked you to apply for it."

"Which I did quite willingly," she felt obligated to say. "Just as I agreed to get hold of whatever data I could to help with his lawsuit."

"Until you realized my plane wasn't responsible for the death of your parents. At which point you informed him your involvement was at an end."

"He told you all that?" she asked in wonder. "Of his own free will?"

"I didn't put him on the rack, if that's what you're asking. But I didn't make it easy for him, either." He faced her. "He's getting help, Anna. He admitted his lawsuit was a desperate attempt to fix blame elsewhere, to deny any possibility that he made a mistake piloting the Seawolf. He's accepted responsibility for the accident that killed your parents, as well as the accident that injured you. And he's checked himself into a hospital."

"Poor Benjamin," she murmured. She suspected Sebastian didn't agree with her rather generous assessment of her brother, but to her relief, he didn't comment.

"Benjamin also told me something else," he continued. "He said you called him months ago, confessing you had feelings for me and that you wanted to tell me who you really were."

"Yes. He gave me his blessing to pursue the relationship. He said he was ready to drop the lawsuit, but recommended I stay quiet about my identity for a while longer. He said it would give the whole nasty business time to die down." She sighed. "But that wasn't the real reason."

"No," Sebastian confirmed. "He had no intention of dropping the suit. Instead he planned on blackmailing you." He lifted an eyebrow. "Something along the lines of—give him the information or he'd reveal everything, perhaps?"

She nodded. "He called on our wedding night while you were in the shower," she said, shivering as she remembered her fear, her panic. "But I couldn't do what he asked. I couldn't betray you, no matter what the cost. I lied, told him that I had the information and would meet him in front of the hotel. I knew the only way to end his incessant plotting would be to leave you. Permanently."

He approached. "Which brings us to the night we made love. Your memory returned that night, didn't it?"

"Yes," she whispered. "I think making love to you is what brought it back."

His eyes darkened. "Why didn't you tell me?"

"Because I was afraid you'd assume the worst. It looked rather damning, especially considering where Benjamin and I were headed the next morning."

"To the airstrip. To examine the computer files."

"Only we didn't get there," she stated bleakly.

"Because I came after you and took a tumble off the mountainside. At which point . . . you made a deal with Benjamin."

Tears started to her eyes. "He told you?"

"He told me. My life in exchange for the computer files."

She bowed her head. "It was one more betrayal. I didn't think you could possibly forgive me."

Disbelief gathered in his eyes. "Not forgive you? For saving my life? For facing your worst nightmare and flying with me to the hospital?" He snagged one of the envelopes from the couch. "Last time you chose to disappear, rather than betray me. Which brings us to our second bit of mail." He held it out.

"The letter I sent you the night of our wedding. But..." She looked at him in confusion. "It's not opened."

"It would seem my new PA isn't quite as efficient as my old one. She saw no urgency in getting this to me. It explains everything, doesn't it? Your identity, why you left, says goodbye."

She nodded, too overwhelmed to speak.

"Tear it up."

"I...I don't understand."

"Get rid of it." His expression grew tender. "Have you any idea why I brought you here?"

Mutely, she shook her head, the tears finally escaping.

"You thought it was to punish you, didn't you?" He touched her then, and it was as though the gates to heaven had opened. He pulled her into his arms, wiping the tears from her cheeks. "It wasn't a punishment. I brought you here because this is where we left off. This is where our marriage was put on hold. And this is where it resumes. We never finished our honeymoon. Now we will."

She gazed up at him, losing herself in brilliant silver-gray eyes. "Do you mean that?"

"I mean it."

"I love you, Bastian. I know it seems that I forgot that for a short time, but I suspect it was self-protection. Leaving you was the most difficult, most traumatic thing I'd ever done. Perhaps that's why my brain short-circuited, refused to allow the memories to return. Remembering would have forced me to leave all over again. And I didn't want to."

He cupped her face. "You listen to me, Anna Kane. And don't ever forget what I'm about to say. You are my life, my heart. Even if there'd been no accident, I would have found you and brought you home. I love you. I'll love you to the end of my days... and beyond. Despite what you said in that hospital, one night as my wife isn't enough. Not for me. Not by a long shot."

"Then let's make it two," she suggested, lifting her face, her love gleaming in her eyes, filling her voice.

He didn't need any further prompting. He took her mouth, worshipping her with an ardor she'd never experienced, sweeping her into a special world of warmth and light and passion... and opening the door to the rest of their lives.

Anna and Sebastian returned to the island a week later, sailing there on a leisurely honeymoon cruise. When they arrived at *Rochefort*, they heard the tolling of bells. From every single watchtower the bells rang, rang in joyous greeting and welcome. And from that day forward they were no longer known as the Bells of Doom, but as the Bells of Destiny, a promise of everlasting love and happiness to any who heard them.

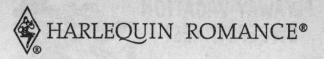

HARLEQUIN ROMANCE®

Coming Next Month

#3379 BRIDES FOR BROTHERS Debbie Macomber
The first book in **Midnight Sons**, a very special new six-book series from
this bestselling author.

Welcome to Hard Luck, Alaska. Location: 50 miles north of the Arctic
Circle. Population: 150—but it'll be growing soon! Because this town is
determined to attract women. The campaign is spearheaded by the
O'Halloran brothers, who run a small-plane charter service called
Midnight Sons. Thanks to them, things are going to change in Hard Luck—
maybe more than anyone expects....

In *Brides for Brothers* meet Sawyer O'Halloran, one of the Midnight Sons,
and Abbey Sutherland from Seattle, librarian and divorced mother of two
young children. Abbey's the first of the women to arrive in Hard Luck—
but she hasn't told anyone she's arriving with kids!

#3380 THE BEST MAN Shannon Waverly
Kayla Brayton remembered Matt Reed as a handsome, self-assured
twenty-one-year-old, and she fully expected a handsome, self-assured
thirty-one-year-old. She wasn't disappointed! Matt was the kind of man
every girl dreamed of, but was he the best man for her?

#3381 ONCE BURNED Margaret Way
Family Ties
Guy Harcourt was strong, forceful and dynamic. He was also irresistible
to women. And Celine Langston was no exception. She had never wanted
anyone as much as him. But she was like a moth caught in a candle's
flame, and once burned...

#3382 LEGALLY BINDING Jessica Hart
Sealed with a Kiss
Jane was a sensible girl—everyone said so. Ten years ago she'd been far
too sensible to run away with the local rebel, Lyall Harding. But now
Lyall was back and the bad boy had grown into a successful businessman.
Was now the time to throw caution to the wind?

AVAILABLE THIS MONTH:

#3375 THE BABY CAPER
Emma Goldrick

#3376 ONE-NIGHT WIFE
Day Leclaire

#3377 FOREVER ISN'T LONG ENOUGH
Val Daniels

#3378 ANGELS DO HAVE WINGS
Helen Brooks

FLYAWAY VACATION SWEEPSTAKES!

This month's destination:

Exciting ORLANDO, FLORIDA!

Are you the lucky person who will win a free trip to Orlando? Imagine how much fun it would be to visit Walt Disney World**, Universal Studios**, Cape Canaveral and the other sights and attractions in this area! The Next page contains tow Official Entry Coupons, as does each of the other books you received this shipment. Complete and return *all* the entry coupons—the more times you enter, the better your chances of winning!

Then keep your fingers crossed, because you'll find out by October 15, 1995 if you're the winner! If you are, here's what you'll get:

- Round-trip airfare for two to Orlando!
- 4 days/3 nights at a first-class resort hotel!
- $500.00 pocket money for meals and sightseeing!

Remember: The more times you enter, the better your chances of winning!*

*NO PURCHASE OR OBLIGATION TO CONTINUE BEING A SUBSCRIBER NECESSARY TO ENTER. SEE BACK PAGE FOR ALTERNATIVE MEANS OF ENTRY AND RULES.

**THE PROPRIETORS OF THE TRADEMARKS ARE NOT ASSOCIATED WITH THIS PROMOTION.

VOR KAL

FLYAWAY VACATION
SWEEPSTAKES

OFFICIAL ENTRY COUPON

This entry must be received by: SEPTEMBER 30, 1995
This month's winner will be notified by: OCTOBER 15, 1995
Trip must be taken between: NOVEMBER 30, 1995-NOVEMBER 30, 1996

YES, I want to win the vacation for two to Orlando, Florida. I understand the prize includes round-trip airfare, first-class hotel and $500.00 spending money. Please let me know if I'm the winner!

Name_____

Address _____ Apt. _____

City   State/Prov.   Zip/Postal Code

Account #_____

Return entry with invoice in reply envelope.

© 1995 HARLEQUIN ENTERPRISES LTD.   COR KAL

OFFICIAL RULES
FLYAWAY VACATION SWEEPSTAKES 3449
NO PURCHASE OR OBLIGATION NECESSARY

Three Harlequin Reader Service 1995 shipments will contain respectively, coupons for entry into three different prize drawings, one for a trip for two to San Francisco, another for a trip for two to Las Vegas and the third for a trip for two to Orlando, Florida. To enter any drawing using an Entry Coupon, simply complete and mail according to directions.

There is no obligation to continue using the Reader Service to enter and be eligible for any prize drawing. You may also enter any drawing by hand printing the words "Flyaway Vacation," your name and address on a 3"x5" card and the destination of the prize you wish that entry to be considered for (i.e., San Francisco trip, Las Vegas trip or Orlando trip). Send your 3"x5" entries via first-class mail (limit: one entry per envelope) to: Flyaway Vacation Sweepstakes 3449, c/o Prize Destination you wish that entry to be considered for, P.O. Box 1315, Buffalo, NY 14269-1315, USA or P.O. Box 610, Fort Erie, Ontario L2A 5X3, Canada.

To be eligible for the San Francisco trip, entries must be received by 5/30/95; for the Las Vegas trip, 7/30/95; and for the Orlando trip, 9/30/95.

Winners will be determined in random drawings conducted under the supervision of D.L. Blair, Inc., an independent judging organization whose decisions are final, from among all eligible entries received for that drawing. San Francisco trip prize includes round-trip airfare for two, 4-day/3-night weekend accommodations at a first-class hotel, and $500 in cash (trip must be taken between 7/30/95—7/30/96, approximate prize value—$3,500); Las Vegas trip includes round-trip airfare for two, 4-day/3-night weekend accommodations at a first-class hotel, and $500 in cash (trip must be taken between 9/30/95—9/30/96, approximate prize value—$3,500); Orlando trip includes round-trip airfare for two, 4-day/3-night weekend accommodations at a first-class hotel, and $500 in cash (trip must be taken between 11/30/95—11/30/96, approximate prize value—$3,500). All travelers must sign and return a Release of Liability prior to travel. Hotel accommodations and flights are subject to accommodation and schedule availability. Sweepstakes open to residents of the U.S. (except Puerto Rico) and Canada, 18 years of age or older. Employees and immediate family members of Harlequin Enterprises, Ltd., D.L. Blair, Inc., their affiliates, subsidiaries and all other agencies, entities and persons connected with the use, marketing or conduct of this sweepstakes are not eligible. Odds of winning a prize are dependent upon the number of eligible entries received for that drawing. Prize drawing and winner notification for each drawing will occur no later than 15 days after deadline for entry eligibility for that drawing. Limit: one prize to an individual, family or organization. All applicable laws and regulations apply. Sweepstakes offer void wherever prohibited by law. Any litigation within the province of Quebec respecting the conduct and awarding of the prizes in this sweepstakes must be submitted to the Regies des loteries et Courses du Quebec. In order to win a prize, residents of Canada will be required to correctly answer a time-limited arithmetical skill-testing question. Value of prizes are in U.S. currency.

Winners will be obligated to sign and return an Affidavit of Eligibility within 30 days of notification. In the event of noncompliance within this time period, prize may not be awarded. If any prize or prize notification is returned as undeliverable, that prize will not be awarded. By acceptance of a prize, winner consents to use of his/her name, photograph or other likeness for purposes of advertising, trade and promotion on behalf of Harlequin Enterprises, Ltd., without further compensation, unless prohibited by law.

For the names of prizewinners (available after 12/31/95), send a self-addressed, stamped envelope to: Flyaway Vacation Sweepstakes 3449 Winners, P.O. Box 4200, Blair, NE 68009.

RVC KAL